# SEX & COFFEE:

## A Bitter Little Time Capsule of Love

## Erika Lee

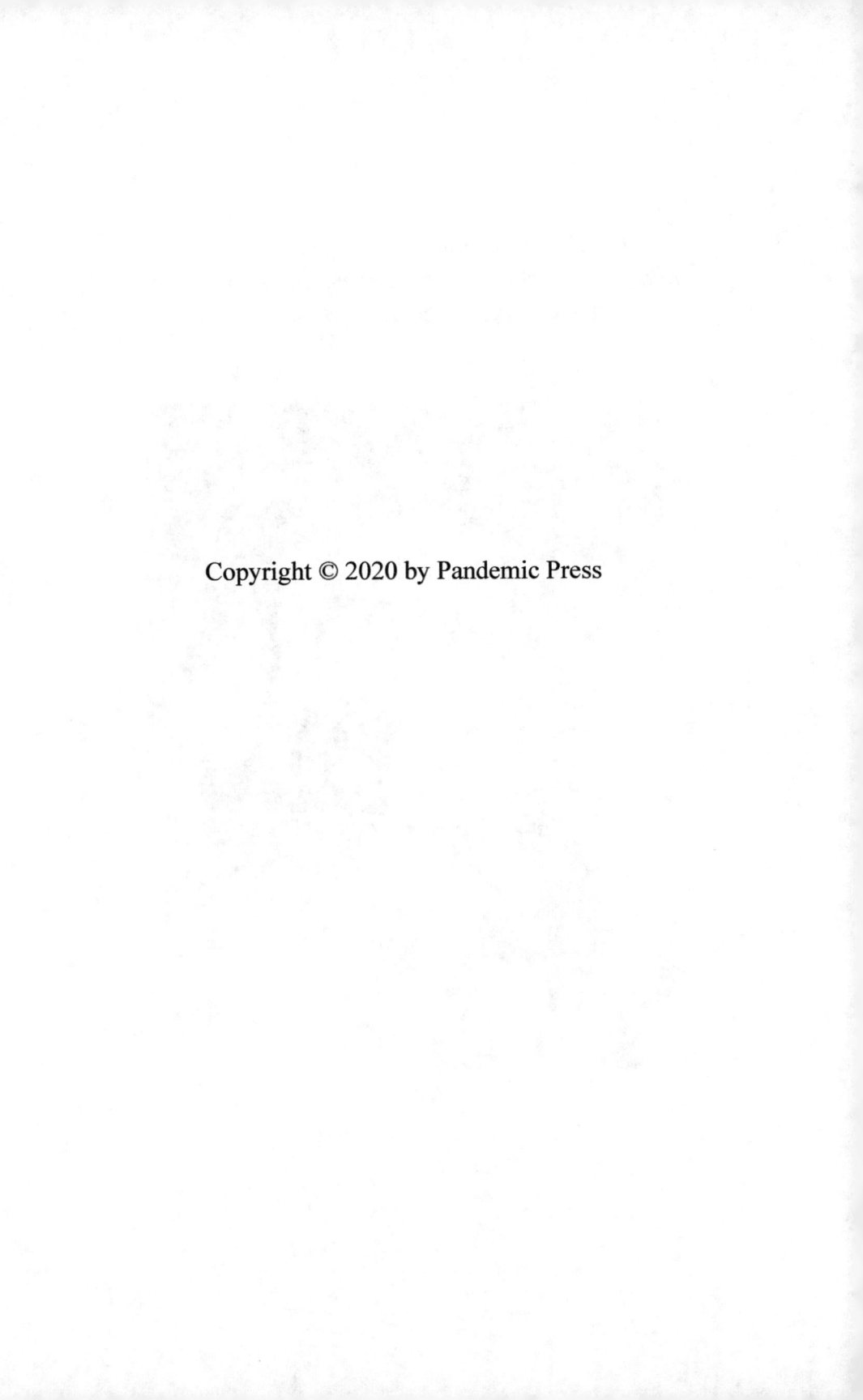

*To all of my brilliant female ancestors who,
against their better judgement and perhaps their will,
had to eat their thoughts, words, and ideas.*

# *Prologue*

This epistolary "slice of life" novel spans twenty five years between September of 1994 and June of 2019. It is woven together as a dual narrative and told from the perspective of star-crossed lovers Destiny and Matthew. The letters written by Matthew are all set in the fall of 1994 when his beloved was away at NYU and he stayed behind in their hometown of Palm Desert, California. The couple had been together less than a year and this was the first time they were apart. Destiny's diary entries span the agonizing twenty year aftermath of their eventual breakup.

# 10♣

*"Ramakrishna once said that if all you think of are your sins, then you are a sinner. And when I read that, I thought of my boyhood, going to confession on Saturdays, meditating on all the little sins that I had committed during the week. Now I think one should go and say, 'Bless me, Father, for I have been great, these are the good things I have done this week.' Identify your notion of yourself with the positive, rather than with the negative."*

—© Joseph Campbell
*The Power of Myth*

**Friday, June 14, 2019**—The Queen Bean Café—Yucaipa, California

My Dearest Matthew,

In my younger and more vulnerable years my father gave me some advice that I've been turning over in my mind ever since. "If you want people to like you," he instructed me on countless occasions over the course of years, "be very interested in everything they have to say. Act like you really care about their lives."

He also advised me to pay close attention to the casual words folks utter when first you meet them. "If you pay close attention," the old man assured me with a twinkle in his blue eye, "people will tell you who they are and what they're going to do. It's subtle but they'll tell ya. Listen."

1

What seemed more abstract than obvious when first I heard it grew explicit as time wore on. Turns out, Pops was on to something. Ornery old bastard made everything about him, lacked empathy, emotional depth and parental instincts, yes. But dude was spot on about many important matters. People do reveal themselves in subtle and not-so-subtle ways early on. Often in the guise of projection.

Of course, I didn't know anything about any of that back then. I was too torn up inside to see past my overwhelming self-consciousness, crippling fear, quick-shifting emotions and all those intrusive, obsessive thoughts. I had nothing to offer anybody except my own confusion. Consequently, I lacked the empathy necessary to conduct myself appropriately in a romantic relationship. For that and the countless times I selfishly betrayed you, I am deeply and eternally sorry. You were the best thing that ever happened to me and I fucked it up.

Regardless of how ugly I may have behaved, please know that *you are the love of my life*. Nothing compares to you, Matt. Trust and believe that I've suffered in untold ways since you left. Thanks to karma, shame and your total obliteration of me from your life. Cleary, I'm dead to you. Carrion flies do seize upon my pale lips in some dark corner of your heart. Your expulsion of me set in motion the darkest night of my soul. There aren't enough adjectives in the English language to adequately convey the depth of pain I've endured and vigorously endeavored to blot out during this vast space between us. My sorrow and bitter regret are as intense today as they were twenty years ago. It never goes away. It never will. You just learn to "live" with it.

Drugs help.

What I owe you, as much as an earnest apology, is a debt of gratitude for the priceless lessons you taught me. Not to say that you're my raison d'etre / green light or anything, but you are the greatest teacher I've ever had. You taught me that there are consequences of our actions and that when you treat someone who loves you like shit sooner or later they're going to walk away and never look back. You taught me how and why to be a better person.

Remember the last movie we saw together? *As Good as It Gets.* Remember what Jack Nicholson's character tells Helen Hunt's? "I've got a really great compliment for you and it's true. You make me want to be a better man." There was so much synchronicity in our last date it's incredible. I wish I'd have known about all of that back then. Synchronicity, karma and the like. Nobody taught me nuthin'.

Matthew Ian Altenberg, I've got a really great compliment for you and it's so fucking true. Losing you made me a better woman. I wish you could see the better woman I've become and could fully comprehend the pain in took to get me here. Losing you was more painful than losing Kay on January 1, 1999. And in case you've forgotten, my name is Destiny Jane Jones. It's been many a moon since we lay our blue eyes upon each other. The last time I saw you was at TGI Friday's in Woodland Hills sitting at a table near the front door with your left arm slung around your pretty new girlfriend. Late '99. When I walked in and our eyes met, you leaned in to kiss her on the cheek then gave me some strange salute.

And so began my dark night.

You're happily married now to that same lovely lady. You have a family, your Ph.D., the suburban-American dream. You must be so proud. I'm proud of you. I too am a teacher. I teach English at a charter school for at-risk kids in the desert. Although not in the way I'd originally imagined, I get to use my acting skills every day. Children make a captive audience. And along with the perfunctory vocabulary and grammar lessons, I teach the value of being a "good person"—a person of integrity—to my students whenever possible. I explain to them the law of karma, citing everyone from Christ to Buddha to Alan Watts, Carl Jung and of course, Joseph Campbell. Our mentor.

In *The Power of Myth* Campbell said to Bill Moyers: *"Freud tells us to blame our parents for all the shortcomings of our life, and Marx tells us to blame the upper class of our society. But the only one to blame is oneself. That's the helpful thing about the Indian idea of karma. Your life is the fruit of your own doing. You have no one to blame but yourself."* So when my students confide in me that they secretly wish to do "bad things," I explain

3

to them that they only want to do those things because they're ignorant of the consequences of doing them.

"If you knew what would happen to you as a result of doing that," I informed a student recently with a twinkle in my blue eye, "you'd think twice. Trust me." Today, I'm a noble benefactor of my community because of you. And because of you, dearly beloved, I can dive into my watery grave having tasted true love if only for a moment in time.

Speaking of taste, thank God for coffee! Yes, I'm as obsessed as ever with my favorite libation. Often it was only the promise of a Venti Cinnamon Dolce Latte with whip and sprinkles that prodded me from my rueful slumber. The courage it took to get out of bed every morning to face the same things over and over was enormous. On many a dark morning, I stared at the ceiling pondering whether or not I should get coffee or a gun to kill myself. Fortunately, the coffee always won. That's addiction for you. Cunning, baffling, mighty powerful. Pops called it "the phenomenon of craving."

Apparently, my addictive impulses were greater than my suicidal ones. Although, I'll admit, coffee's never tasted as good as it did when you were mine. Harley's. Gloria Jean's. Espresso 2 a Tea. The Coffee Connection. Jazz & Java. Java the Hut. Lala Java. Those were the best iced mochas and cappuccinos I'd ever have. Everything since has paled in comparison. Not long ago, in fact, I was a barista at the most popular coffeehouse in Palm Springs knowing full well that even their European iced mochas couldn't compare. Because you weren't there.

I'll never forget those Java the Hut quad-shot iced cappuccinos I'd get right before Robert Rosenblum's art history class at NYU. Pure, unadulterated liquid crack. I'd literally be vibrating through his lectures on the Pre-Raphaelite Brotherhood. Vibrating, wishing you were there to quiver with me. Thank goodness I still have all the beautiful letters you wrote while I was in New York to give me strength.

How cruel that hindsight has to be 20/20. Why in the hell can't foresight be so? I wish I could go back in time and do it over. I would have never left NYU after less than a semester. I would have waited patiently for your eventual arrival. I would have taken therapy seriously and made a real effort to get to the bottom of my debilitating emotional problems rather than projecting them onto you. We would've never moved to L.A. I would have never cheated on you and we would have never broken up. But that's not what happened and now, a secret sorrow haunts my days and nights. Few know anything of it. Only those closest to me have the slightest clue.

As I said, drugs help.

Especially, really strong coffee.

These days, I'm strictly the served rather than the server of espresso, etc. And as I nurse the 16-ounce cup of medium roast before me in between decadent flakey nibbles of a pain au chocolat, I can't help but wonder what in the fuck I was thinking twenty five years ago when I did those appalling things to you. Was I deranged? Delusional? Duplicitous? Depressed? Dumb as driftwood? Whatever the perplexing root cause of my aberrant behavior—you, nevertheless, are and always will be my great American tragedy.

Love Always,
Destiny Jones

P.S. I never fucked Billy.

***

**Monday, September 5, 1994**

To My Love, Destiny,

I just arrived at JFK. I'm looking out the window at my plane. It's a 767. The same we had five days ago. A beautiful five days ago. It doesn't seem that long. It seems like just a few hours ago we were walking through this airport, getting our bags at the baggage claim and worrying about getting a cab. My cab driver took the Queens Midtown Tunnel. I saw a cemetery which was probably the one you were talking about. It was cool!

I miss you already. I wish you were here. That goodbye on the street was rushed. Maybe it worked out for the better. Our hug and kiss seemed too short. Anyway, I just want you to know that I love you. I love you with everything that's inside of me. Body and soul. Although you're not with me now in the flesh, you're alive inside my heart and will continue to be so long as we're apart. This makes me want to cry.

Stay strong. You'll be fine. I'll be fine. I know you're going to make it. Just focus on the matter at hand: your school and December 22, 1994. I trust you. Please trust me. Everything's going to be fine. By the way, we were ripped off by the first taxi driver. I don't know why he took the route he did—the Triborough Bridge, FDR Drive, etc. I only had to pay a $27.25 cab fare this time around. Granted, the highway had less traffic today. Our cab driver didn't take "the most direct route."

It just occurred to me that by the time you receive this letter it'll be Friday or Saturday. This distance is going to suck a dick. Because of the distance we're going to have to be consistent with our letters to each other. That way there'll only be a brief moment in time between them. Catch my drift?

I'm wondering what you're doing right now. Talking with your roommates? Walking around the Village? Unpacking? Crying? Reading? Eating? Getting stamps? Finishing those postcards? Thinking of me? Feeling lonely? I'm thinking of you and will be for the next three and a half months, and the next five years, and on and on. I love you, Destiny Jane Jones. I can't wait until we can live together in NYC. We'll love it. Just hang in there. If you have an extra postcard send it to Mike and Diana in Seattle. They'd appreciate it. It's going to be a long flight to Los Angeles.

We sure did take a lot of pictures. It'll be fun to look at them with your parents. I'll send them as soon as they're developed. We had a lot of fun at the Met, in Times Square, and seeing St. Patrick's Cathedral, Trump Tower, Rockefeller Center, The Plaza Hotel, Central Park, etc. I'll hold these memories close to my heart forever. Especially the next three and a half months while you're away. They just announced my boarding call, so I have to go. I'll continue this in the LAX terminal. Think of me often. I'll be thinking of you.

### Six hours later...

I just arrived in L.A. It's 6:00 p.m. here and 9:00 p.m. in NYC. Six hours. That's all it's been. The flight was alright. It was about five and a half hours total. I was pretty hungry so I ate some barbeque chicken. The meal was good. It was just a small portion. I'm sitting here eating a personal pan pizza from Pizza Hut and drinking Pepsi of all things. Just five days ago we were here together. Smiling, farting and fretting about New York. It's funny how time and memory play cruel tricks in our head.

I had a great time with you in New York. I'd like to come back there to live, no doubt about it. I hope you get acclimated and comfortable quickly. I want you to like New York City. I don't want you to be lonely, sad or depressed. That really tears at my heart. I can't tell you how much it hurts me to think that right now you're depressed. I know this is what's best. It just hurts. I'm really missing you. We'll be fine. You're going to like New York. Just be patient. I hope you call tomorrow when I visit your folks. Remember, 7:00 p.m. your time. I hope you do. It's just weird to think that you'll receive this letter on Friday or Saturday. I'm / we're accustomed to sending a letter and having it arrive just a day or two later. No longer! I'm going to relocate to my gate.

I'm sitting at Gate 49B. The very one we walked through when we arrived here in L.A. at 7:30 a.m. on Thursday, September 1, 1994. The terminal's dead compared to when we were here. The major departures for the day have all left. My layover is just about an hour. I read lots of Joseph Campbell on the plane. It made me think of you. Reading *The Power of Myth* cheers me up. It's kind of strange. I guess it's because Joseph Campbell seemed like a real positive person with a hopeful message.

The reason I always think of you when I read it is because you once told me it was that book which inspired you to do what it is you're doing now—following your bliss. Remember, you're in New York to do something greater than simply go to school. It's the first step toward a way of life. Something you know you have to do, whatever it takes. Keep that in mind. Don't let the ugliness of the city get to you. Look for the beauty. There are nice people there. There are mean people there too just like in Palm Desert. They're everywhere.

You made a lot of friends at Barnes & Noble. Think of how many friends you made at College of the Desert. Those people aren't exactly friendly. You're in an environment at NYU that's the best possible setting for meeting people. You're going to be interacting with people like never before. You'll get to know them easily because you'll be acting with them. Remember how many people you met at your first acting class at COD? I have a point, don't I? Surely one of your roommates will be cool enough to drink iced mochas with. Not as cool as we are, of course. Just try to enjoy yourself and imagine the life that's ahead of you and us.

I want you to find the best iced mocha in the Village so that when I join you there in January we'll have a new place to go. That one by the Tisch building doesn't quite cut it. I don't think it's our speed. Stay vigilant. Also remember that we'll hit all the jazz clubs when I'm there. We'll have a lot of fun. We'll see shows and milk that wretched, puke and piss stained city for all it's worth.

Hold steadfast to your convictions. Namely, your love for me. Nothing to worry about on this end, dear. I'm yours and yours only. Don't worry about bimbos in my classes. All I see is you my sweetest, dearest, most beautiful, thoughtful, insightful, observant, talented, and slated-for-success future wife. I also want you to tell me about every illustrious celebrity/musician/artist you see, meet or listen to at NYU. Because let's face it, you will see, meet and/or listen to them. That's the place to be. You've done good, darling.

Well, I've said all that I can think of here in L.A. so I'll pick up my pen and write the final chapter of this agony and ecstasy when I get to my house in... yuck... Palm Desert. Visiting New York with you has made my desire to be there stronger. Remember: these three and a half months are going to sail right on by just like our first ten did. Don't worry. I'm sending this letter out tomorrow instead of today because I can't find any stamps or envelopes here in the terminal. I love you. Goodbye for now.

### *Five and a half hours later...*

I'm finally home. It's 11:35 p.m. I'm exhausted. To start, I got home an hour late. When we took off from L.A., about two minutes into the flight, the right propeller cut out. It just stopped. We had to turn around, land at LAX and ended up getting transferred to a SkyWest flight an hour later to Palm Springs. Needless to say, I and everyone else on the plane was scared shitless. My dad was at the bar when I arrived. We got the luggage and drove home. I called your dad first thing. He asked how you were, and I said, "a bit nervous" but that you'd be fine. I'll see him tomorrow at 4:00 p.m. Hope you call.

I'm about to set my clock and go to sleep. It's blinking and has to be re-set for some reason. This about sums up my day. I hope yours was a little better. Somehow, I doubt it was. Remember always that I love you— completely, truly, devoutly, deeply, and astronomically! Keep your chin up. Stay strong. Think of me and most important of all: keep on truckin'.

I love you, Destiny Jane Jones.

Sincerely,
Your boyfriend and future husband,
Matthew Ian Altenberg

P.S. I can't say it enough: I love you and am counting the days until you return on December 22nd. Please write ASAP. I'm sure you already have.

\*\*\*

*"The usual hero adventure begins with someone from whom something
has been taken, or who feels there's something lacking in the normal
experiences available or permitted to the members of his (or her) society.
This person then takes off on a series of adventures beyond the ordinary,
either to recover what has been lost or to discover some life-giving elixir.
It's usually a cycle, a going and a returning."* ©

## Saturday, February 27, 1999

Dear Diary,

NEWS FLASH! Matthew stopped by to "talk" on Thursday night, and I know he called the day before but didn't leave a message. Can you believe it? I star sixty-nined a hang-up I got at about 5:30 p.m. The call was blocked. I know it was him. It had to be. He must've been responding to the two crank calls I made to him on Monday.

During a lull at work I called Bookstar in Woodland Hills, asked for him and when they put me on hold, I hung up. Don't know why I did it. Just to fuck with him I guess. I'm surprised he responded so quickly. I was talking to Cynthia when my call waiting beeped.

"Someone's calling on the other line," I told her. "Hang on a sec." I clicked over. "Yes?" There was a pregnant pause and then...

"Destiny, it's Matthew."

My heart tripped a beat.

"What do you want?"

"I'm outside. I want to talk to you."

"Hold on." I clicked back over to Cynthia. "Matthew's at the front gate."

She gasped then growled then demanded that I get rid of him. "He just wants to fuck you!"

"Hold on," I told her then clicked back over to him. "You still there?"

10

"Yes."

"I'm on the phone. Call me later." I hung up on him. He never called. Whatever he has to say I don't want to hear it. I'm not going to be rejected by him ever again.

On Friday, I sent him another spiteful note reiterating what an asshole he is and that I never want to see him again. "Believe that" was how I ended it. Even better, I opened the note with: "Rejection sucks doesn't it?" It felt so good to finally express that. I've suffered intensely ever since he left. Over a year now. I can't bear to suffer anymore. Mom's been gone three months and I've got that grief to deal with, too.

Still, I can't help but wonder if he'll keep coming around. Though it soothes my battered ego that he does, I'm terrified to see him. I know I'll be hurt again. He'll come over, we'll have empty awful sex, he'll reassure me in some vague way and then he'll leave. I won't hear from him again for weeks or even months. It's an agonizing cycle. To think that we'd been so close, best friends, once upon a time and now—this is what's left. Him showing up unannounced to use me for sex. To think that I've been reduced to a warm wet transitory hole for this person who once declared his eternal love is difficult to swallow.

Speaking of Hole, what does Courtney say on *Live Through This?* "I want to be the girl with the most cake / I love him so much it just turns to hate / I fake it so real I am beyond fake / And someday you will ache like I ache." I hear you, girl. That's exactly what this is—love and hate. To truly hate someone you had to truly love them first. Logically speaking, you can't hate someone you didn't at one time love deeply. Hate by any other standard is a fallacy. Pure delusion. Whether it's love or hate these days I'm not quite sure. All I know is it hurts like hell.

Last night while he and I were enjoying a couple espresso martinis at the Bourgeois Pig in Hollywood, Stephen made an interesting observation about Matt and I. Stephen's my rebound boyfriend. We met when I transferred to Bookstar in Studio City from Barnes & Noble in Northridge to get away from Jonathan. That's another story. Stephen's a few years older than me and the spitting image of that fine dude who played Sue in the movie *Swingers*. Same hot temper, too.

I told Stephen that Matt had stopped by the night before but that I didn't let him in. Of course, I omitted the part about the crank calls I've been making to his place of employment. After a couple drinks and some obligatory gossip about our Bookstar coworkers, Stephen started to loosen up. He drunkenly described Matthew and I as having a "secret relationship."

"What does that mean, 'a secret relationship,'" I asked him.

"You know what it means."

"No, I don't know. Tell me. You're the one who brought it up and I'm intrigued." I started to think he was fucking with me which he likes to do.

"It means that regardless of how much time passes or how your lives change the two of you will silently sustain a…secret relationship."

"But I rarely ever see him."

"Doesn't matter."

"I've seen him what…maybe three times since he broke up with me over a year ago."

"Three times, eh? Good to know."

"So how can I have a 'secret relationship' with someone I never really see?"

"Other than those three times."

"Please don't start. We're having a good time."

With that strange, borderline creepy look he gets, his pitch-black hair slicked back away from his pitch-black eyes, Stephen smirked then said, "You don't need to see each other, Destiny. Even though you clearly still do since he stopped by to fuck you the other night."

"I told you, I didn't let him in. I hung up on him. You can ask Cynthia."

"Yeah but you wanted to let him in. All the fucking way."

"Stephen, please. Not tonight."

"You probably only didn't because Cynthia stopped you."

My espresso martini was beginning to take hold. "I really don't ever see him, so I'm confused."

"It doesn't matter. You only need to fall asleep."

"Fall asleep?"

"Perchance to dream. And since you're still in love and always will be, it'll continue. He'll fuck you in your dreams."

***

## Monday, March 29, 1999

Dear Diary,

My God, what do I do about Stephen? Linda came up last night for her 22nd birthday and the three of us went to Barnes & Noble in Calabasas. I had to return the suitcase Jonathan loaned me for our recent trip to Europe. When he sees us, Jonathan abandons his post at the cash wrap and sprints across the store in order to introduce himself to Stephen who was in the music department listening to George Michael's 1987 classic *Father Figure*. Although Jonathan was visibly nervous, Stephen stayed surprisingly cool. Dude loves to fight, and I assumed meeting Jonathan would present him with the perfect excuse to do so. I know he doesn't believe that Jonathan and I didn't have sex when we were in Europe. I'm telling you, we absolutely did not. Not even close. I may have fucked him all the time behind Matthew's back but those days are over. Across London, Paris and Milan we traveled and not one time did that thick Arab sausage pierce my dainty lips. Even though we shared a bed the entire trip.

Impressive, right?

I was repulsed by the thought of him going up in me and getting all crazy like he does. Stephen can't fathom this and I get it. I wouldn't believe him if the roles were reversed. The fact that I even went to Europe with a former lover is pretty weird. But how do you turn down an all-expenses paid European vacation? You don't and I didn't. After watching Kay die slowly I needed to fly far away.

After Barnes & Noble the three of us (in two cars) headed straight for our home away from home—The Bourgeois Pig. Linda and I arrived first. Stephen rolled up shortly thereafter. As we waited in line to order our drinks my worst nightmare begins to unfold. Stephen's favorite blonde barista emerged from the back and you'd better believe he noticed. I thought his eyes would pop right out of that fat head when he saw her. My heart sank into my socks as it always does on these occasions.

I immediately brought the sickening scene to Linda's attention. Elbowing her in the side I whispered, "See, see! There he goes. That's his little bitch, the one I was telling you about. Motherfucker. That's what the fuck I'm talking 'bout right there." It was all I could do to stay in my skin.

"I see it." Her green eyes widened, appearing especially fixated on Stephen's every move. We hadn't even ordered yet and our night was ostensibly over. My good mood quickly evaporated into the aromatic atmosphere. Once this happens, once those dark, intense, inexplicable feelings take hold as a knee-jerk reaction to something my boyfriend du jour says or does, forget it. I'm toast. Completely unable to recover. It can take hours, sometimes days, for me to return to emotional homeostasis. It's perplexing and painful.

The first time I recall feeling this way was the summer before my 4th grade year. Pops and I took a blistering hot drive from Cabazon to the Tyler Mall in Riverside to see a matinee of *Annie*. I was obsessed with the film and its soundtrack at the time. I even had the wig which I proudly wore to Ms. Schindler's class at Hoffer Elementary.

Pops and I had a lovely time until we were about to head back home. As we stood outside the theater looking at the movie poster, my father commented on how "pretty" he thought Ann Reinking was. In a flash, the concrete floor beneath me fell. I was besieged by a visceral rage that I couldn't have articulated if I wanted to. It rendered me utterly distraught, and I spent the entire drive home choking on it.

In retrospect, what made me so angry was in that instant, I saw my otherwise cold, inexpressive, often abusive father show a scintilla of "affection" toward someone other than my mother, other than myself, both of whom he mercilessly beat on occasion. The whole thing felt a lot like betrayal. Little did I know back then, but the feeling I felt standing in front of that movie theater would become all too familiar as I progressed through life and relationships.

After ordering our coffee Stephen, Linda and I got a table as far from the espresso bar as possible. It didn't matter though. That dreadful feeing I simply can't shake already possessed me. For a good hour, I berated Stephen for his disrespectful pattern of behavior. Anytime we'd go into the Pig—which was often—and she was there, I could never relax. His focus would always be on her, if only peripherally, and never completely on me. "You know," I said with palpable sarcasm, "if you find her so captivating, by all means don't let me obstruct the golden bliss that awaits you."

Of course, he played dumb again, denying my perception.

"What are you talking about now?"

"I'm talking about the fact that you're clearly attracted to blondie over there. I'm sure Linda would agree."

"I saw it," Linda said. "You like her." Thank God my best friend since middle school was there to back me up. Yes, jealousy is tacky. I can hear my mother's raspy voice now, "Destiny Jane, that's so uncouth." But goddamn it, what he does on a regular basis is uncouth. It's downright rude though he's not alone in his misconduct. Every boyfriend I've ever had was guilty of this. Even Matthew. But with Stephen, a serial blonde ogler, I couldn't keep quiet any longer.

Linda, a cute blonde herself, pointed out that what seems to annoy me more than anything is that he continues to deny his behavior. The two of us finally got him to admit that yes, he does find her attractive. No shit. Although I already knew this, it pierced my heart to actually hear the words uttered. Much like it did that hot summer day in 1982. Yes, this is my pre-existing complex: a profound feeling of female inferiority. This is so reminiscent of my early days with Matthew. The feelings that overtake me are so intense, so uncomfortable, and never seem to wane regardless of whose arm I'm on.

Needless to say, the night ended without Stephen. After enduring my intense verbal attack, he told us that he was going to score some cocaine from his bartender buddy Vince at the Norwood. Here we go again. The downward spiral descends even further. Though I tried to get him to stay he refused. I finally gave up and told him that I couldn't have anything to do with him on drugs. The last thing he said to me was, "Just forget you ever knew me."

I let him go.

Linda and I now have this little bet going to see how long I can go without calling him. I always fucking call him. Even after my mom died I had to call him. He didn't have enough class to call and see how I was doing. Yet, he'll say stuff like, "Don't make me live without you," and "I can't think about you when I masturbate because the memory's too painful," and "I want you to be my last."

Delusional romantic bullshit.

I think he's being transferred to Bookstar at the Beverly Connection, so God knows what'll happen to us if we no longer work together. The proximity factor's always been why we've gotten back together. Proximity and unbearable boredom.

***

**Wednesday, September 7, 1994**

To My One and Only Destiny,

I'm sitting here at home alone. Things are different. I can't just call you up or drive to Barnes & Noble and see you on your lunch break. I miss you. I just finished chapter one of *The Power of Myth* ("Myth and the Modern World") and the subsequent journal. My dad went to Norco to drop off Mark and talk to the high school superintendent about getting him in school. He guesstimated that he'd be back at 7:00 p.m. My car's in the shop so I'm stranded here all day. I'll do my homework and try to get used to being without you. I'm listening to Prince (*Thieves in the Temple*). I decided to put him on while I wrote your letter for the obvious reason that it makes me think of you.

Nick left a message today asking how things went in New York and to tell me he'll be in the desert this weekend. Of course, he didn't think to leave his number (*1999* just came on) so that I could call him back. Sounds like Nick, huh? I'm going to call Jamie later, too. I'm looking forward to your call.

I've relocated to the toilet to do my thing. I had to order a Papa Dan's pizza. There's no milk or anything else in this house. A funny story on the Phil front. Our two favorite people (guess who the second is) went to (*Gett Off* just started) Lollapalooza. You guessed it: Ron. Those two freaks went to Lollapalooza! I'm sure Phil soiled his shorts seeing The Breeders live. That's funny to me, and I knew it would give you a chuckle as well. Billy told me about it.

I think you and I are going to be just fine. Don't you? I'm sitting here shitting, wishing you were here laughing with (*Erotic City* is about to start) and talking to me. I miss you. I hope everything with your roommates work out. They seem cool and all. I also hope your bedding, towels, etc. come today. That mattress of yours looked pretty heinous. I hope the odor dissipates quickly. I'm also positive your period will arrive soon enough, Saturday probably, so don't fret. *Delirious* just began.

I got fifteen points (the maximum) on my first journal for Myth and Legend and turned in the second one today. Things are looking good there. Our first paper for Decision Making & Advocacy is due this coming Tuesday (the three advertisements). Shouldn't be a problem. *Little Red Corvette* just started. How did the job interview go? It's a brand new Barnes & Noble opening up in the Village? I'm really excited for you! You're/we're going to have fun in NYC.

The phone just rang. It was Nick. He asked how things went. I told him they went well. I didn't talk to him very long because he had to go to class.

At the tail end of my conversation with him, there was someone calling on call waiting. It was Jamie. I talked to him and told him about me quitting karate class. He took it well. He said that if I had to take a leave of absence that was fine with him. He understands. *I Would Die 4 U* just started. So that's good. I was a bit worried about him getting upset or whatever.

I can't wait for your letter to arrive. It probably won't get here until Friday or Saturday. That's too long to wait. This long distance shit sucks, huh? *Raspberry Beret* just started. I wonder what you're doing right now. It's 7:30 p.m. your time. Twenty-four hours until you call here tomorrow. I can't wait. I think I'm gonna get going. I have a lot of homework. Stay strong. I love you. I miss you. *Kiss* just started. Perfect timing.

Your best friend.
Your partner in crime.
Your most loyal fan.
And future hubby,
Mr. Matthew Ian Altenberg

***

*"The secret cause of all suffering is mortality itself, which is the prime condition of life. It cannot be denied if life is to be affirmed. Human suffering is a principle theme of classic mythology. The only true wisdom lives far from mankind, out in the great loneliness, and can be reached only through suffering."* ©

**Tuesday, March 30, 1999**

Dear Diary,

Today was weird. During the supervisor's meeting at work Andy announced that Stephen was being promoted to lead bookseller and transferred to Bookstar at the Beverly Connection. Jennifer will be stepping into his shoes here. I thought I'd be sick. And not because I was passed up for promotion by Jen. As everyone smiled and clapped for them, I sat there stiff as a corpse. Poker face in full effect. I couldn't move. I was paralyzed with all variety of impending doom.

When I got up to go to the bathroom, I caught a glimpse of myself in the mirror. My cheeks were flushed as fuck. The shock of the news actually turned my cheeks a deep rose. Makes sense. As I sat there listening to it all, I could feel a slow burn begin to rise inside of me. It started in my toes and made its way up to my scalp. It was all I could do to keep from sobbing. I must've been in denial up to this point about him leaving. Now it's real. Why do I even care? This is the same guy that smacked me in the face and knocked me out of my own bed after having sex. As he's curdling inside me, I said something that angered him so he backhands me and kicks me out of my own damn bed.

When I got home from work today, my face still ablaze, Cynthia called. In one breath I blurted out what happened. "Stephen's being transferred to the Beverly Connection store. It's really happening."

"Good. You two need to be separated."

"You're probably right but it still hurts."

"It can't hurt any more than the way he's treated you this whole fucking time, Destiny."

"Right? No, you're absolutely right."

"Goddamn right I'm right."

"The other thing," I told her (which was a variation of the truth), "a friend of mine (Linda) saw him loitering at the Pig on Sunday afternoon flirting with his favorite barista." In truth, as a branch manager of Bank of America, Linda's able to track Stephen's purchases since he banks there. She told me that he'd used his debit card at the Pig on Sunday. I didn't want Cynthia to know that I was taking it so far as to financially stalk him. She'd really flip out.

"Destiny," she said in that shrill Cynthia tone, "if he's going to fuck around there's nothing you can do about it. Obsessing all the time ain't going to do a fucking thing to stop him."

"Fuck, Cynthia. I know. I can't seem to help it."

"You've got to ask yourself: is this the kind of relationship I want? With someone who's drunk all the time, violent and unstable? Don't you think you deserve someone better than Stephen?"

I wasn't sure how to answer her.

"You're right," I finally said. "You're absolutely right."

"You're just addicted. You're addicted to love, Destiny. Stephen's your drug of choice right now." Considering her long history with intoxicants this was beyond an ironic statement.

"I never thought about that way."

"Be more attracted to what's good for you."

And there it was. Cynthia might be a one-note actress, but she sure is brilliant at delivering the cold, hard, unfettered truth. Sometimes I appreciate it. Often I don't. In this instance she might be on to something.

"I'll try," I replied before saying goodbye.

I think I felt so awful today because it appears as though another person I love is leaving me. First Matthew, then Mom and now Stephen. We've been going out off and on for almost a year now. I realize he's not perfect, but he's helped distract me from the torture of losing Matt. I'm afraid of how this move will change us. Every time we've reconciled it's because we work together.

I felt so uncomfortable sitting in that stupid meeting. I even forgot about the whole blonde barista thing. It looks like he'll be going to the other store in a couple of weeks. I'm really dreading it. I'll miss him around there in spite of his bullshit. When things are good he's a fabulous diversion. Funny, smart and fucks like a swarthy beast. I'll definitely miss the sex.

But I'm sticking to my guns and not calling him.

After I got off the phone with Cynthia, I felt so neurotic that I almost drove to the desert to see Linda. At La Tuna Canyon I changed my mind and turned around. I then proceeded, out of curiosity, to drive to the Beverly

Connection to check out the competition. An Asian girl with a name tag reading "Annie" gave me the key to the restroom. Could this be the same slut Matthew told me he's been dating? Other than that, I saw no real threat in the lame bunch that was there tonight.

As I weaved my way up Laurel Canyon back to the Valley, I noticed something scribbled on my dusty windshield that I hadn't noticed until the waning sunlight hit it just right. It was a heart with the letter "U" inside of it and the letter "R" off to the side. "Love You, Richmond." Did Stephen scrawl that on there today? I bet he did. Why the fuck can't he just say it to my face?

Last night on the phone, Linda said that she thinks Stephen cares about me but that he doesn't know how to handle it. I think he cares, too. He's just so screwed up. I'm afraid of losing him as someone to pass the unbearable time with. If we're being really honest here, that's what it is. I'm terrified of being left alone in this apartment. It's like a tomb. A cold and lonely little tomb.

***

**Friday, April 2, 1999**

Dear Diary,

Billy drove down from Santa Barbara last night to see his friend's band Lint play at Luna Park. It started off shitty when Stephen failed to show up as planned. We took separate cars to the venue and I rode with Billy, but we lost Stephen along the way. He never made it, and I was a neurotic mess. I couldn't enjoy the band one tiny bit. All I could think about was my psycho love.

After the show I asked Billy if we could try to find him. I had a sneaking suspicion he might be at his favorite dive bar, the Norwood. So we left Luna Park headed in that direction. Sure enough, there he was standing in the corner of the room with a pool cue in one hand, a Guinness in the other and a Marlboro Red dangling precariously from his bottom lip. A lip which happened to be agape in shock when the two of us strolled in.

"What the fuck happened to you?" I said, making a furious beeline straight for him.

"Oh, hey!" said Stephen, plucking the fag from his bottom lip.

"What the fuck? Why'd you ditch us?"

"I thought you guys ditched me."

"C'mon, man." He was bullshitting and I wasn't having it.

"Seriously. I couldn't find Luna Park and figured you guys were fucking with me."

"Bullroar," I snapped.

I have this thing, this gift, you might say. I know when someone's lying to me. Can't explain how it is that I know, but I do. Probably has something to do with being raised by one of the most skillful and prolific liars God ever created—my mother Kay. And this motherfucker was bullshittin' through his tobacco stained teeth. He just wanted to go to the bar.

"How long have you lived in this fucking Valley? And you don't know where Luna Park is? Please. I may have been born at night but it wasn't last night."

Liars are the worst. And their lies, the ultimate red flag. No matter how "nice" they can be, once you catch someone in a bald-faced lie that's your cue to exit stage left pronto. Of course, that's not what I did. I let it slide again. He was the nice Stephen now; the one I fell for from the start. A pleasure to be with. Funny, insightful, romantic, easy on the eyes. He reminds me of my father when he was a young man. Same exact look except Stephen doesn't wear glasses.

In spite of the rough start to our evening the three of us ended up having a great conversation. After we all got a little table in the middle of the joint, Stephen walked over to the jukebox, dropped some coins inside her and played the song: *How Soon is Now?* by The Smiths. I'd never heard it before. Not that I recall anyway.

22

"If you want to know what's it's like being me," he told Billy and I upon returning to the table, "listen."

*I am the son*
*And the heir*
*Of a shyness that is criminally vulgar*
*I am the son and heir*
*Of nothing in particular*

*You shut your mouth*
*How can you say*
*I go about things the wrong way?*
*I am human and I need to be loved*
*Just like everybody else does* ©

He proceeded to open up and explain why he "needed" the Norwood. He said that he likes to go there when he's in pain, which is often. "You know, to disappear and get into the suffering," he confessed.

"But you're better than that," said Billy.

"I tell him all the time. He doesn't believe me."

After Billy left I went back to "the cave" aka Stephen's house to wait for him while he conversed with his friend Vince. As I sat on his unmade bed, I noticed one of his journals lying on the floor just screaming to be read. I've flipped through it before. All darkness and gloom. Non-sensical ramblings about hating life and wanting to die. This time, I actually found some stuff he'd written about moi—near exact quotes of things he's said to me. He wrote that I was the thing that "completed him." His "missing half."

When he finally came home, we watched a couple episodes of *South Park* then got naked. It's usually Stephen who likes to be a little rough when we have sex but this night, he was an unusual lover. More submissive and gentle than dominant. Perhaps the fact that Billy and I went out of our way to find and comfort him put him in the mood. The lovely things I read certainly put me in the mood. Whatever it was, the boy was down to please.

I let him come inside me again and again. He usually pulls out and blasts the walls with it. Not tonight.

I slept like a baby.

Oh shit, I almost forgot. I had an audition today in Westwood and ran into Rick Roberts there. I mean *Richard Gunn*. He's going by "Richard Gunn" these days now that he's an actor, too. We went to high school together. I used to sexually harass him for fun in Spanish class. Senior year, he discovered the magic of theater and made the conversion as I had in the 10th grade. I was the one who convinced him to pursue acting as a career. And there he was.

We chatted for a bit and of course, I had to ask about Matthew. I knew they were friends. He said that he talks to him whenever he calls their place for Rick Levy. When we broke up, Matthew moved in with Pat and Rick about five miles away from me. I asked him what Matthew's been up to and he replied, "Oh you know Matt—school, school, school." Rick mentioned nothing about a girlfriend, but I don't know if that's something you discuss with someone's ex you run into at a commercial audition.

Poor Cynthia. She was kind enough to accompany me to the audition and had to sit in my car for over an hour while I did my thing. Luckily, she brought a book to read—John Sarno's *The Mindbody Prescription*. She swears by it. She's always in some kind of pain and claims that's why she needs all those Somas. I just wish she wouldn't take them and drive. Especially when I'm her passenger.

\*\*\*

**Tuesday, September 13, 1994**

To Destiny, My Love,

I just got home from school. I'm not feeling well. I'm lonely and depressed. The stress of your news coupled with the conclusion of our conversation today are really hurting me. Sometimes, I feel like I've failed you. You tell me that I've never made you feel beautiful, and I wonder if I can ever recover from this deficit. I think I can and will keep trying. You tell me it's impossible. I disagree.

I look at my pictures of you and you're always smiling. It's easy to see which ones are a pose and which ones are genuine happiness. What a beautiful smile you have. It makes me so happy to see you smile. I wish I could conjure that genuine peace, happiness and security you have in me at that moment all the time. Your joy is always tenuous and fleeting which saddens me.

This pregnancy has really got my emotions topsy-turvy. I feel a bit disconnected from you due to the 2,500 miles that separate us. I really wish I could be there to hold and comfort you. This hurts me deeply. It hurts me deeply that I can't touch the woman I love and tell her things will be alright and have her feel the depth of my sincerity. All I can do is talk to you on the phone and try to imagine what you're thinking, feeling and going through.

I'm so happy you found a friend to confide in. Christina sounds awesome. A painter studying psychology? How cool. That makes me sleep a little easier. It's 1:20 a.m. your time. You're fast asleep, I imagine. I'm hoping our conversation didn't upset you too much. I worry about how upset you can get seemingly out of the blue. I hope it was just a temporary reaction to all the stress. I'm a good person but often feel that I'm not. I feel inadequate. It's a terrible feeling and must be how you've felt. It kills me to think that I made you feel insecure with my careless words and wandering eyes.

I hope you don't think I'm being impersonal about the abortion. I'm getting that feeling from you. I also get the feeling you think I don't care about what's happening or just want you to get rid of our child as soon as possible. I didn't make up my mind immediately. I gave it a lot of thought, and unless we want to set aside everything we've worked for we have to get an abortion. You tell me how you're sick and depressed and lonely all the time. I'm really worried about you. I don't know exactly how you're feeling. All I have to work with is what you tell me. I know you well enough to know that you're confused, lonely, miserable, and disillusioned right now (all of this *not* including the pregnancy). I just wish I could be there to give you strength.

However, right now neither one of us can use the other for strength. Not like before. The only strength we have is our ten months together, our love and devotion. I'm always with you, Destiny. My love is always with you. Although you're not by my side right now, you're always with me. I can feel you always. We've bonded in a way that is special. We'll work through all of this.

Granted, your end is a bit more difficult than mine but you can do it. I have complete faith in you and your ability to succeed. You have what it takes though I know you wonder. I know you're plagued with doubts about yourself but you needn't be. You've got everything going for you. Beauty, brains, talent, heart, soul. When in doubt, just think of me and keep on truckin'.

I doubt myself sometimes, too. I wonder if I'll rise above my father and put myself through school in NYC. I believe that I can. I've seen my strength through you. I wouldn't be half the person I am today without you. I'd still be where I was a year ago, lacking the experience and insight that you've instilled in me. You always talk about how I've changed you. Think of how you've changed me! All this talk of how different I am now—it's because of you. Everything I have now is because of you. I'm so proud to think that you're in NYC fighting all of your demons to make something out of yourself. You're my hero!

When I got off the phone with you, all I could think about was how you never think it's possible that I love you as much as you love me. It rips my heart in two. Why is this so inconceivable? Where do these doubts come from? It perplexes me. Sure, we have some issues we need to work out before we move to the next level of our relationship. That's normal. Unfortunately, we can't work them out over this distance but we will work them out. It's time to let go and trust the other person.

Unfortunately, we've come to a detour. I hate to downplay the pregnancy, but it was the only metaphor I could think of. We have to move through this. You and I have too much to lose over all this. What we have can overcome anything. Just stay strong. God, I love you. All this is very hard for me, Destiny. I feel so helpless. Please try to see my point of view. I'm the man who loves you.

Tonight, I'm going to say a prayer for us. To help us work through our personal problems and to get through this pregnancy come what may. People like us rise to bigger and better things so hang in there. December 22nd only seems far away.

Always yours,
Matthew

***

*"In the Tristan romance, when the young couple has drunk their love potion and Isolde's nurse realizes what has happened, she goes to Tristan and says, 'You have drunk your death.' And Tristan says, 'By my death, do you mean this pain of love?' –because that was one of the main points, that one should feel the sickness of love. There's no possible fulfillment in this world of that identity one is experiencing. Tristan says, 'If by my death, you mean this agony of love, that is my life. If by my death, you mean the punishment that we are to suffer if discovered, I accept that. And if by my death, you mean eternal punishment in the fires of hell, I accept that, too.' Now, that's big stuff. What he is saying is that love is bigger even than death and pain, than anything. This is the affirmation of the pain of life in a big way." ©*

## Friday, April 16, 1999

Dear Diary,

I just awoke from a nap by a phone call from Pops. I was dead asleep when the piercing ring startled me awake. Dazed and confused, I flung myself out of bed, staggering over to answer it. "Hello." I could barely get the word out; I was so exhausted.

27

"Destiny, what are you doing?"

"Taking a nap, Pops. What are you doing?"

"Oh, nothing. I hope I didn't wake you."

"It's ok. I was having a bad dream anyway. What's going on?"

"I was just worried about you. You seemed like you were in a bad mood yesterday when you left."

"Did I?"

"Seemed that way."

"I'm fine, but I appreciate your concern."

"I sure do love you, D."

"I love you, too."

I wasn't up to discussing the troubling information I learned after leaving him yesterday. In fact, the bad mood Pops was referring to as I left Palm Springs wouldn't actually roll in until *after* I got back to L.A.

I met up with Nasario and Stephen for coffee at Starbucks in Studio City. Nasario and I used to work together at Barnes & Noble in Northridge. Now he works with Matthew at Bookstar in Woodland Hills. I enjoyed our visit even though Stephen was acting strange. When I asked him what was wrong, he said he hadn't drunk in two days and was desperately craving alcohol. It was hard for me to believe he hadn't had anything to drink considering his perspiration reeked of booze.

When I took Nasario home after coffee, I brought up Matthew. I couldn't help myself. He was the only one I knew who had regular contact with him since they worked together. I told him that Matthew had stopped by my apartment a fortnight ago, but that I didn't let him in. "I'm sure he just wanted to fuck me," I said.

Nasario giggled with unease. As we made our way from Studio City back to Northridge, I delicately probed him about whether or not Matthew had a girlfriend.

"I don't think so," Nasario said but in the same breath mentioned a girl named Bernadette coming into Bookstar to meet him.

*Bernadette?!* Upon the mere mention of a name, I hit the brakes which jerked us forward. The person behind me honked.

"What does she look like?" I asked him, trying valiantly to conceal my horror as my heart spiraled straight down into my G-string. "A short Asian girl with a pixie haircut."

"*Another* one?"

Nasario didn't respond. I'm sure he didn't know what to say. I was beginning to perspire. I fought to stay calm and not get us into an accident. *Ten and two* I repeated like a mantra in my whirling, swirling head. *Ten and motherfucking two.* The bad mood had official set in.

I mean, what's up with this Asian shit? In our 4 ½ years together the notion of Asian girls never creeped its way into the conversation. Not even when we were having sex and I'd encourage him to fantasize about other girls aloud did he even allude to a taste for Asian pussy.

See, I knew it. I knew he was hiding shit from me.

Before I dropped him off at home, Nasario reiterated that he didn't think Matthew had an "official" girlfriend. I'm sure he could sense my overwhelming distress though I tried my damnedest to hide it. I don't know if I believed him or not. He acted a little strange about me asking in the first place, though I showed absolutely no emotion whatsoever. Poker face in full effect like the supreme actress that I am.

Inside, however, it was an entirely different matter. I felt batshit crazy. Utterly unwell. Matthew's clearly dating, quite possibly fucking, earnestly attempting to get over me as I write this very entry. I wonder if and when I'll ever get over it; this living, breathing hell. I've been in hell since last winter and there ain't a brighter day in sight. I've been thinking about him incessantly since he showed up at my front gate three weeks ago. God knows how much I'll owe on star sixty-nines this month.

29

I had a great conversation with Sarah Shourd, a coworker, about it all at Pane Dolce in Sherman Oaks today. We each got one of their incredible non-fat iced cappuccinos and a pair of chocolate-dipped madeleine's. She thinks Matthew will keep coming around despite my rejection of him. I even told her what he'd said during our last conversation, the night mom died: "Even if I were married," he assured me over the phone, "I'd still have sex with you, Destiny." Sarah thought that was an awful thing to say. It really flew all over her.

"Never let yourself be used by someone like that. *Ever*. Do you understand me?" She didn't like his statement one tiny bit and told me not to have any contact with him whatsoever for six months. I was taken aback by her extreme aversion to his admission.

"*Total silence*. Don't even call his store to look for a book. *Nothing*. And if he does call or come by and you're caught off guard just say: 'Matthew, I can't talk to you.'"

Of course, I'll never call or go see him. I mean, she's right. No more calling his work, asking for him then hanging up. I'm never going to drive by there again looking for his green Civic or even see or talk to Pat or Rick. It's going to be like it was last year at this time. Maybe a good solid chunk of zero-contact is exactly what I need.

My God, I do sound like an addict.

I just get so angry when I think about the way he abandoned me and how, when my mom was dying, he was off having a great time with a couple Asian whores. I hate him and know that I can never have anything to do with him again. We'll never be "friends." Forget it. We were never friends in the first place. I jumped on his virgin dick way too fast that night in the Desert Fashion Plaza parking lot only to wake up the next morning to the news that River Phoenix had died of an overdose on the sidewalk in front of the Viper Room.

We were never friends.

There's no escaping it, is there? My destiny's fated, isn't it? Like running into Rick Roberts of all people at that commercial audition. I can't believe I recognized him so quickly. Thank God for Stephen. Despite what he thinks, he's not a transitional boyfriend. Maybe if he keeps ogling blondes everywhere we go he will be. We had the best sex last night. I came so hard I actually broke down in tears. It was as if the force of the orgasm caused an eruption of emotion to pour out of me. I woke up this morning with red marks all over my arms. So worth it.

Speak of the devil, Stephen just called. He asked me if I wanted to "do something" this evening. Of course, I do. He said he'll pick me up at 8:00 p.m. Bye for now!

### *A couple hours later…*

Well, that was a shit show.

After he called, I got dressed to the nines. Red halter tank top. Tight black skirt. Brand new heels. Even some red fucking eyeshadow. At 7:50 p.m. I went outside to wait for him. It was too hot in this apartment. After fifteen minutes, I went back inside to see if he'd called. Nothing. I go back outside for another fifteen minutes. No Stephen. I'm getting pissed at this point, so I call him and leave a message: "It's 8:30, where are you?" I go back outside and wait some more. Now I've had it. I take off all my clothes and jump in the bath. When I get out of the bath there's a message from him: "Guess I missed you."

I can't fucking believe this.

Then the phone rings. I answered it curtly, "What?"

It's Linda. Two minutes later call waiting beeps and I click over. It's Stephen. He's a total asshole to me.

"Oh, you're gonna be spiteful and not let me in," he snarled.

I explained that I was in the bath, but he continued to give me shit. I asked him if he wanted to come back over.

"No," he snapped, so I hung up on him. I'm sure he flew right out the door to the Norwood. To top it all off, today was his last day at Bookstar #1837. We didn't speak the entire day. We only exchanged a long glance at each other upstairs in the breakroom. As a reflex, I shot him a disgusted look before storming out.

This will be the perfect test now that I won't be seeing him at work. I think this time I'm really going to wait it out. If he truly misses and wants to see me, he'll show up. I'm so tired of always being the one to smooth things over. It's exhausting.

***

## Saturday, April 28, 1999

Dear Diary,

Stephen and I are back together. Linda called him last night but he didn't return her call until five o'clock Sunday morning. Apparently, they ended up talking for an hour or more. His story to her was that he feels like I'm better off without him, and that he has a real problem communicating. He also told her that he couldn't stop thinking about me.

I swore to her that I wasn't going to call him, but last Sunday I found myself eaten up with passion once more and did just that. I called him at work and told him, "I hate it when we fight." He agreed and was very cool to me. He called me back later in the day and we talked more. Of course, he asked if he could see me. You *know* what my answer was. I'm not good at "no" when it comes to boys I'm addicted to. We've spent every night together since.

Last night after work we had drinks at the Broiler with Billy who came into town to see *Cabaret* with his friend Ashley. Linda's coming up tonight to sleep over. Hopefully, there won't be any problems.

### *24 hours later…*

What a crazy fucking night Linda and I had. Never again do we go anywhere with Stephen. Linda arrived at 10:30 p.m. and we rode with him to the Pig. I could tell he was in one of his moods even though three hours earlier on the phone at work he was fine. At first everything was copacetic. I ordered my triple mocha with whip and cinnamon dust. Linda had her iced Americano with heavy cream. Stephen got his usual espresso martini. When it comes time to pay, Stephen looked at me and said, "You gonna stiff me again?"

And that was the spark that set our night ablaze.

We went at it for a good hour or so in front of poor Linda. It escalated to the point where he spat in my face and slapped my hand away as I reached out to touch him. Our disturbing fight culminated with him screaming at me to *"Fuck off!"* as his espresso martini spittle spattered on my glasses. How did we get to this point? I suppose his ire was sparked when I made an off-handed remark about finding another date. He was annoying me in the way that only he can, so I flipped the bitch switch.

When his friend joined us, dude made a comment about how pretty my eyes were. I flung my head around so that my nose was square with Stephen's and told him that he should learn from his friend about how to treat a girl. But he was over the edge by this point, making both a scene and an ass out of himself.

Meet scary Stephen.

When he told me to "fuck off," I'd had enough. I jumped up, told Linda I'd be right back and hustled my ass back to the payphone by the restrooms to call Jonathan. When he answered I said, "Hey, it's me."

"Well, hello 'me.' How are you?"

"That's cute and I'm shitty."

"What now?"

"Linda and I are at the Pig with Stephen. He's gone off the rails. We all rode in his car and now he's flipping out."

"When should I come get you?"

"Are you sure? I'm sorry about this."

"Right now?"

"As soon as it's convenient for you. Maybe a little sooner. And thank you. Seriously, I appreciate it." I wasn't about to call a cab or wait for psycho boy to chill his ass out. I was done.

When I returned to the table Stephen said to Linda, "Tell her to use the money she owes me to get a cab," and he left. I told her that Jonathan was on his way. Thirty minutes later when he arrived, Linda noticed Stephen's car in a shadowy corner of the parking lot. We got in Jonathan's Civic and they both see Stephen. I didn't but they did. We began to leave and he started following us.

I'm freaking out in the backseat thinking I'm going to be shot while Linda keeps checking behind us from the front seat to see if he was still there. We finally decide to pull over at a Chevron station. Stephen followed us in. Linda jumped out of the car and ran over to talk to him while Jonathan filled up his tank. Five minutes later, Stephen screeched over to us. His passenger-side door flung open and Linda jumped out. She ran over and got back in Jonathan's car. Stephen then screeched out of the gas station and into the night.

"What the fuck?" I asked her.

She said he didn't say too much, only that he was visibly angry and upset. She made him promise not to hurt himself and to call her. He told her he would, but I seriously doubt that'll happen. We all know what a fantastic caller he is. *Not.*

On a brighter note, Linda convinced me to call Matthew today. So, I did. I couldn't help myself. We conversed for about an hour and it went well. Come to find out that Annie chick did show up the infamous night on the Santa Monica pier after I departed. She even brought some friends. He said she stayed a while then left. And the Bernadette thing, he said that he went out with her a few times but they had nothing in common. Doesn't sound like too much is going on in his life.

It didn't seem like he wanted to see me. Nevertheless, I told him he could call anytime and that he needn't worry about me being a bitch. My whole purpose in calling him was to apologize for the way I'd been acting and for the vicious nature of my little notes. He was nice to me. At first I wasn't sure if he wanted to talk. I was hoping we could get coffee together, but I guess it's best that we just talked on the phone. I think it was a mature move on my part.

I definitely won't be mentioning it to Sarah Shourd.

About Stephen. As much as I care for him, I can't keep going through this. It's heartbreaking to see him act like that. He gets so out of control. Intellectually, I know I have to stay away from him; that this is a hopeless, bad scene. But try telling that to my voracious heart. And aching pussy. Day before yesterday, we had the hottest sex. We spent time in bed afterward talking, laughing and making fun of our coworkers Philip and Joan. He even imitated them fucking. I almost died. I'll never look at the Schmeltzinator the same again.

Linda was right. Our fights seem to be getting more frequent and intense. I still don't know what he was trying to do by following us. I'm actually surprised he did that, although it was in the direction of the Norwood.

***

## Wednesday, September 14, 1994

My Love,

It's been a shitty day. I'm tormented by that gut-wrenching pain I've felt many times before when you say: "I can't be with you anymore." I know you don't really feel that way. You told me that you've consulted your NYU friends on this and they all agree— "Matt has a problem." I may. I haven't completely understood all of this since the beginning. Which is why I've decided to see a therapist. I really want to know whether I have a problem or not. I know this particular "problem" is especially hard for you to endure.

Stay with me. Give me a chance to make it right. Things will change. I hate to hear you so upset. It really breaks me in two. And be careful with your new friends giving you advice. They don't know me; they don't know you; and they don't know the entire situation. I never wanted to get into all of this—our problems—while you were away. There's too much distance between us and dragging all this out over the phone is detrimental to our relationship.

I know you haven't been ignoring our other issue. Do you think you can just break up with me and still carry our child and think that I'm going to dismiss my love for you over all this? Impossible. You have to talk to me, Destiny. It's the only way. I know you hate me right now. I know my voice makes you furious, but you're going to have to set all that aside. Both of us have some issues we need to work out before our relationship moves to the next level. Mine are obvious. But in my defense, I've had no support and no authentic communication. That's why I'm going to see a therapist.

I feel sick. Before, it was easy to drive to your house or go into Barnes & Noble and see you. Now, I can't. And you have someone back there who doesn't know me telling you that I'm sick and twisted. Did I disown you when you had problems? Never. We both have problems. I love you just the same. Let's face it, Destiny. You're never going to find anyone as good as me. We're too close. We both understand each other completely. We share the same beliefs and emotions. We have virtually the same goals. We're compatible. We're both slated-for-success. What more do you need? You need me right now and I need you. Yes, I need you!

Why are you pushing me away? Are your emotions intensified because of the pregnancy? Yes. Are you miserable, confused and disillusioned in New York City? Absolutely. Do you miss me so much it makes you cry blood? Of course. Do you feel completely alone? Undoubtedly. These are all things I'm aware of and understand. You don't want to break up with me; you're just pushing me away at a time you need me the most. Who's going to tell you you're an incredible woman and actress if I'm gone? Your parents will but it's not the same. We're right for one another and that's a fact. I refuse to let you go.

I know everything that's happening to you right now is overwhelming, but you will get through it. You're tough and you're a survivor. Look at everything you've been through prior to New York. You're going to let that shitty city swallow you? New York isn't going to challenge you in a way

36

that you haven't been challenged before. Think of what it is I'm talking about. Everything you've gone through with your mom. The staggering heartbreak and disappointment. You've got all the tools to make it, Destiny. You're the one who'll rise above all this. I'm extremely proud to say that you're my girlfriend. Please don't push me away.

Your loyal and steadfast friend,
Matthew Ian

***

*"In Plato's Symposium, Aristophanes says that in the beginning there were creatures composed of what are now two human beings. And those were of three sorts: male/female, male/male, and female/female. The gods then split them all in two. But after they had been split apart, all they could think of to do was to embrace each other again in order to reconstitute the original units. So we all now spend our lives trying to find and reembrace our other halves." ©*

**Thursday, June 3, 1999**

Dear Diary,

NIGHT FROM HELL! I don't want to bore you with all the messy details of what's transpired between my last entry and now, but let's just say that I didn't see or hear from Stephen for almost a month. As always, I was the one who had to call. And the only reason I called was because I wanted to tell him about what they did to me at Bookstar, accusing me of all sorts of things and forcing me to quit.

And here's the worst news of all: after a little probing over the phone last night Linda admitted that Stephen came on to her last Friday when he and I were in the desert. She said that when they got done grooving on the dance floor at Muriel's and realized I was gone, she allegedly said to him, "This is bad what we've done."

He allegedly replied: "Why? I mean, I might have thought about fucking you but then I forgot about it." And when they were up all night "talking" back at her apartment, he allegedly said something to the effect of, "I don't understand why she's upset," as Linda proceeded to explain it to him. He allegedly told her, "She's upset because she knows I'm attracted to you, too." All of this per Linda, my alleged "best friend."

I remember meeting her that day in the fifth grade. It was my first year at Precious Blood Elementary in Banning. Pops wanted me in a "better school" and figured that a private Catholic school was the answer. We weren't Catholic but they didn't discriminate. Money talks regardless of which God you pray to. I learned that lesson early.

The day she and I met we'd been dropped off at the same bus stop and walked home together. The bus I rode home every day from school also transported students from Central Elementary who lived in Cabazon like me. She only lived a couple of blocks from my house. We were virtually inseparable after that even though she was four years my junior. I was in the 10th grade when I discovered she was pregnant. Twelve years old and pregnant. You can imagine my shock. I didn't think she even knew what a penis was much less where it went.

When Linda disclosed to me how she handled the events that transpired at her house after she, Stephen and myself returned from Muriel's nightclub I thought I'd be sick. It was almost like she was bragging about him hitting on her when she said to me, "I don't want to sound conceited, but I know he would've fucked me."

*Huh?*

I'm so hurt. Is that something that a "best friend" is supposed to say to you? Is this normal? I had to get off the phone with her and confront Stephen immediately. When I called his house, motherfucker actually answered. I went right into what she'd told me, and that spineless coward *denied* it!

"You're telling me that my best friend is a liar?"

"Yup," he replied. I then proceeded to ask him over and over again why he'd lied to me for a year. He said that he hasn't lied to me, that he loves me.

*Is this love?*

When I told Blanche about everything that'd happened and all the shit Linda told me, she replied succinctly, "I'm sorry, Destiny. That's not a friend. That's a slut."

\*\*\*

**Saturday, June 12, 1999**

Dear Diary,

Yesterday was the big 26 for me. I feel so old. It's straight downhill from here. I went to Tom and Cynthia's for a little birthday celebration. Cynthia had a chocolate cake, some balloons and a gift for me. We ate chicken pita sandwiches with Caesar salad from Gelson's. It was divine. She even had an ice blended mocha with whip from the Coffee Bean waiting in hand when I arrived. Now that's a friend. We watched tv for a bit, and then I went home to change clothes for my 10:00 p.m. date with Jonathan.

The two of us went to the Pig. After a brief argument in front of Claudia and Keith when Jonathan mentioned it was my birthday, even though I asked him not to, we started to enjoy ourselves. He listened as I lamented about how disturbed I am over the whole Stephen / Linda incident. We concluded that Stephen's a white trash piece of shit and that Linda encouraged him. Jonathan theorized that while the two of them were downstairs at her place watching *Schindler's List*, Linda was likely rationalizing how she could fuck him and get away with it.

"For all you know, they've been fucking for months," Jonathan suggested.

"Oh my God."

"I've been suspicious ever since the night I picked you two up."

"If the roles were reversed and the Ferrari Jew, Linda's recently divorced boy toy, said those things to me," I hissed at Jonathan, "I'd look at him and say, 'Hey, douchebag. You're Linda's dude and that's out of line.' Bitch said nothing close. Little slut. Blanche was right.

When I told cousin Diana about it on the phone yesterday, she said that Linda was more to blame than Stephen.

"Women don't do that to other women," she said. "Once trust has been broken, that's it. I'm sorry, honey."

"I can't believe I was so stupid."

"To be old and wise, you must first be young and stupid."

I know Diana's right, but I'm still confused as to how I should feel about Linda. I really love her. She's like my little sister. She should have just told me she was having feelings for Stephen. I would have likely said, "He's all yours." Never in a million years would I have dreamt her capable of such betrayal. And not just betrayal but a heartless, arrogant duplicity. My God, I was naïve. So fucking blind. Just like with Stephen, I ignored the bright red flags that were constantly flapping in my face.

And him, he's dead to me. I'm sure I'll never see his sweaty alcoholic ass again. I should've listened to him that day in receiving at Bookstar when he said point blank, "You don't want to fuck with me, Destiny. I'm an asshole."

He warned me.

I should've listened.

Well, I don't care how fucked up he is there's no excuse for what he did—humiliating me like that. I could never forgive him. And of course, he didn't acknowledge my birthday yesterday either. He didn't even acknowledge my mother's death in January, so why the hell would he acknowledge my stupid birthday? Surely he hasn't convinced himself he's innocent. Although returning that film of our infamous night at Muriel's was an admission that he's a liar since he'd denied having it.

I even asked sweet Claudia last night when Jonathan and I were at the Pig: "You saw us together almost nightly in this joint. Do you think he really liked me?"

"Of course," she replied without hesitation. "I thought he was in love with you. I still do, but…"

She didn't complete her thought.

Even Jonathan said he thinks that Stephen probably loves me.

"He just can't handle it," he said.

Whatever that means. I can tell you one thing—never again will I pick up a phone and dial him. I don't care what happens. And I mean it this time. *Never*.

Jonathan and I ended up having a pretty good time. Afterwards, we came back to my apartment because he wanted to see the pictures of my crazy night in Palm Springs with Stephen and Linda. He couldn't figure out why Stephen attempted to steal them and didn't think the content was *that* titillating. Although, he did seem intrigued by the one of Linda and I kissing at the bar, as his dick began to slowly rise whilst examining it.

After the pitstop at my apartment we drove across town to his. Despite the fact that he's "dating" that girl Noelle with the stinky snatch we had sex. I actually wanted to.

Here's the thing. It's something I've never discussed explicitly before, but I've been known to get pretty fucking wet at the thought of doing "bad things" sexually. By "bad," I mean things you're not supposed to do. Risky things that might be ridiculed in the eyes of society at large. Cheating, for example. Like when I started having sex with Jonathan while I was living with Matthew. Jonathan and I were coworkers at Barnes & Noble in Northridge at the time and thus, proximity brought our voracious loins together.

Or the time I fucked that hot homeless boy in the very bed I shared with Matthew: Curtis. Whom I also met at Barnes & Noble in Northridge. Talk about bad. This would be the first cock I'd have that wasn't Matthew's. I'm not going to lie, that was one of the most epic orgasms on record. I remember being on all fours, my ass curled as high as I could arch it, begging him to fuck me deeper. I even got down on my elbows to make more room for his barely legal dick. As I rubbed my swollen clit furiously, the boy managed to get that perfect thing even deeper inside of me, squeezing my hips tighter with every stroke. His cock thrust so deep, I'm certain I felt it in the back of my throat.

Pretty bad, right?

I was so horny on this particular Tuesday in 1997 because I was ovulating. My throbbing pussy oozed that clear jelly-like substance all day at work. That's how I know when I'm ripe. And it's during this one-to-two-day ripeness that a stiff prick feels the best. During ovulation, either side of my lower abdomen begins to ache worse than any menstrual cramps I've ever had. Only a big dick in need of release can quell the radiating pain. On this particular evening, while Matt was at work, the boy had exactly what I needed. When Linda so famously said, "Sometimes, you just got to have something in there," this is what she meant.

It's a literal phenomenon.

The fact that Matthew could've walked in on Curtis and I mid-orgasm that night only intensified the pleasure, and I slowly started to come. This was the peak of sexual excitement for me. Sex as a criminal act. The best orgasms aren't the ones that hit you like a Mack truck. Au contraire, they're the ones that build slowly; that rise up from your ankles to your calves, knees and thighs until rolling right up inside your cunt via your clit where the ultimate explosion takes place. The longer the rise, the greater the pleasure.

As I began my slow ascent, the boy's cock seemed to swell even bigger. Pulsing, pulsing, pulsating. He was rising, too. As my contractions began to increase from the ecstasy our unlawful deed invoked, I could feel my cunt grip his cock in tight, quivering flutters.

"Come inside me, baby." I groaned. Anything less than that would diminish from the complete and total wrongness of the act. The uttering of my command was all the boy needed to trigger a loud, guttural "Fuuuck," as a warm deluge was unleashed inside of me. My pussy continued to contract as he came, sucking him all the way up into me.

Talk about sick and twisted.

Last night with Jonathan, I figured that a hearty orgasm was exactly what I needed. I mean, shit—I just found out that my best friend has been fucking my sometime boyfriend behind my back for God knows how long. Months, maybe. I needed a release. You would've needed one, too. And the kind of release I speak of can only be had by being very bad. Cheating with someone was almost as bad as cheating on the one you love. This particular night, being bad meant lying on my back, my legs spread wide, rubbing my aching clit gently counterclockwise as Jonathan's fat cock squeezed in and out of me. With two strokes he was already squealing with adolescent pleasure.

"I love this pussy," he whined.

Aside from maybe Phil, Jonathan was the only guy who, while he was fucking me, would thrash my pussy in a frenzy of excitement as if he'd never met a warm cunt before. This tendency of his, every time we had sex, repulsed me to the point of coming my brains out. There's something so completely wretched about watching a man lose his mind and his dignity when enveloped inside a warm wet one.

The fact that Jonathan was also fucking someone else made the act that much more erotic because I wasn't supposed to be doing it. It was bad, rebellious, immoral. Deciding to make the most of this fact, I made him tell me all about how good her pussy felt while he was buried inside of it.

This is all so very wrong, right? But that's exactly what gets me off. I've even been known to fantasize about someone who repulsed me. This sort of fantasy can be a huge turn on. I know I'm not the only one who feels this way. Sam admitted that she has similar repulsive fantasies.

Anyway, it was an okay birthday.

\*\*\*

## Thursday, September 15, 1994

My Love,

How are you doing? I hope you're alright. I feel shitty. This pregnancy stress is really taking its toll on me. I feel like my stomach is constantly upside down. All I want to do is sleep. I have no appetite. I can hardly think. I hope you fare better.

I had two horrible dreams last night. The first one was the worst of the two. We were at NYU. I was taking a class there and the instructor was Martin Scorsese. We were happy for a moment and then you started ignoring me, telling me to get away from you, and you left me on the street all alone. The school looked nothing like NYU, and the city was real strange. After you left me, I wandered the streets for a while before making my way to your dorm. When I got to the top there were strange people in your room. I didn't recognize any of them. They told me you had died.

"Let her go," one of them said in a virtual whisper.

The second one was peculiar, too. I dreamt that I was at some strange house with your mom. I wandered into some back room and found you there cowering in a corner. You were trying to hide from me. I asked what you were doing back in the desert but you didn't answer. You just handed me a money order with strange writing on it. It was for $1,000 and made out to your dad. You told me to give it to him then left with your mom.

The dream flashed to me handing the money order to your dad and telling him what happened. Then it cut back to you arriving back at the house. You were acting real strange. You'd dyed your hair a deep purple and your mom did something freaky to her hair, too. I asked you what was happening and you told me you'd dropped out of school to live back here until we could leave together in January. The stress of the distance between us was too much for you to handle. I remember being happy but confused. Then I awoke. It was 9:00 a.m. I had to get ready for school.

I slept with you last night. Your picture anyway. It's not the first time I've done that. I miss you, Destiny. I've decided not to call you for a couple of days to see if you call me. I feel like I'm always the one reaching out. Writing this is very painful. I hope you've released some of those negative emotions and are able to think a little more clearly. I know how angry you can get.

What you said yesterday hurt me like nothing you've said before: "I've talked to people and they think you have a problem." That fucking hurt. I'm not sure if it's true. It could be. That's why I'm going to a therapist. My father told me today that he's going to one for this Susan crap. I told him that I wanted to see this man too because there are things about myself I'd like to better understand. I'm hoping this gives you some security. I just feel like time and again I've been told that I'm fucked up and had better change.

Saying to me yesterday, like all the previous times, that you couldn't be with me anymore made me sick with pain. We've come so far and to lose it all now doesn't seem right. I realize this is a hard issue, but am I really *that* fucked up? I don't think so. We've never been able to talk about this in a constructive manner, so that's why I'm going to see someone that may be able to help me and in turn, us.

Please stay with me. I'm the best guy you'll ever find and you know it. I realize that I've done things that hurt you. Mostly, the stupid things I've said to you out of ignorance. I've been hurting from them ever since they came out of my mouth. You always say how important honesty is. I've been honest. But it's a catch-22. When I'm honest, you often attack me. All those comments you make really hurt. I know you're in pain but so am I. I don't need you to put me down to feel the pain from all this. I've forgiven you for many things you've said to me.

I was thinking last night about that time at Stacie's when you told me you'd been a prostitute at the Erawan Garden Hotel. That night really upset me and I've never voiced it. We've talked ad infinitum about how I've "rejected" you, made you feel ugly, etc. This is all true and I'm not trying to downplay it. I'm just trying to find level ground here. I was hurt initially because of what you told me, and I believed you, because you'd never told me that before. Then when you told me it was a joke, I got angry. It wasn't funny at all.

Do you remember how I reacted when you finally told me you'd been fucking with me the whole time? Talk about rejection. What did I say to you? I said it was alright, and that I still loved you, and that nothing you or anyone could tell me would make me feel any different about you. You never seem to remember me saying that. Do you now? I was hurt that you never said, "Matthew, that was a nice thing to do."

Another event I thought of is when you told me in the jacuzzi that you'd had an affair. How did I react *that* night? Do you remember, my love? Again, I said it was alright. I asked you who it was and why you did it. Then you told me that was a "joke," too. Yet still, I went to hug you. How many people when they believe that the person they love more than life itself has slept with someone else goes to hug their best friend? Does any of this count for anything?

Have I cheated on you? No. Is there any doubt that I won't? I would hope not. I'm with you, Destiny. Yes, I'm a bit fucked up and need to understand myself better. Jesus Christ, I'm only 20! Cut me some slack. This is my first rodeo. I think I'm doing pretty good all things considered. Everyone looks at and thinks about other people. What was that story you told me about Robert from Denny's? You fantasized about *him* while we were making love? Why? You told me he repulsed you. That fucking ripped my insides in two, but I forgave you.

Look at everyone we know: Stacie and Jim, Nick, Phil, Carrie, etc. These are people that have thoughts and act on them. Have I really done that much? I have a side to me that's immature and needs to be examined, it's true. I'll work it out. Did I ever say you were fucked up when you'd hit me? What about that time you threw 7-Up in my face? I tried to show you love instead, putting my emotions aside. I've never said, "I don't know if we can make it, Destiny. I think we should end our relationship." I've always been optimistic, steadfast and willing to work things out. You've told me you don't think you're capable of such things. I disagree. I've seen you turn the other cheek and forgive. Forgiveness never ends.

One thing I'm really worried about is you talking to your new friends. I hope you don't put too much stock in what they say. They don't know anything about me, who I am, or what we've been through. Am I like most guys? Am I a selfish, egocentric, dishonest egomaniac who's insensitive to your needs and emotions? Hell no. Did I tell you to get out of my life when it was clear you wanted something from Nick? You've never really talked about it with me. I think you're ashamed of that whole episode. I never felt that you wanted him over me, but there was something more than "nothing" there. Have I ever let you down when you needed something? No. I scraped and clawed my way through it all for you.

Stand by my side, Destiny. Why would I go through all of this if I didn't really love you? If I wasn't serious about our future? Thousands of miles away and enduring this hell. We'll work through this and see brighter days, I promise. Just hang in there. Every relationship has its tests. You've been in two relationships that never got over the first hurdle. You and Jemel were doomed from day one. You and Phil never got anywhere because he's totally incapable of honesty and self-reflection. Do you want the same thing to happen to the relationship you love and cherish most?

Please hang in there, darling. We'll pull through this difficult time. Look to the end of the tunnel. Look to the light. Do you see it? I sure do. It's bright, and white, and beautiful. Just like you. Take my word for it. Trust in me and we'll progress to things so incredible it'll take your breath away.

*"One thing that comes out in myths is that at the bottom of the abyss comes the voice of salvation. The black moment is the moment when the real message of transformation is going to come. At the darkest moment comes the light."* (© from *The Power of Myth*)

I've seen the transformation in you, Destiny. I've seen it in myself. Just hold on, have faith, and you'll see it, too. Actually, you always have. Remember when God entered the room? I'll never forget you telling me that story. You have a beauty that's so timeless, so infinite. I'm praying you'll see it soon. It's there. Believe me. Believe in me.

Your best friend,
Matthew Ian

P.S. I hope you like the flowers. I sent them out today. They should get there tomorrow. Let them heal this pain of ours and be a symbol of the love that binds us closer together until we meet again in December. Stay strong, my love. *Stay strong.*

***

*"Well, it's certainly true in life that the greatest hell one can know is to be separated from the one you love."* ©

**Thursday, July 22, 1999**

Dear Diary,

Keith and I have been inseparable since last Sunday night when we took ecstasy together at his apartment in Silverlake. Yes, I'm talking about Keith aka "Spider-Man" from the Bourgeois Pig. Barista extraordinaire. "Spider-Man" was Stephen's nickname for him because he's always doing these gravity-defying tricks behind the espresso bar.

And yes, I'm also talking about the drug ecstasy aka MDMA aka methylenedioxymethamphetamine. I remember everybody talking about it in high school. They described it as a "non-stop orgasm." With such an enticing description, who wouldn't be intrigued enough to at least try it?

Keith's best friend T, who lives two floors above him, scored us four hits from some chick that frequents the Pig. T, short for Thomas, is a 40-something barista / ecstasy enthusiast who suggested that Keith and I do it together. He was so kind to even offer Keith suggestions about how to make the most of the experience.

"Daddy," he told Keith, "the key is lots of sensory stimulation. Strawberries, orange juice, dark chocolate pudding, massages, prolonged penetration." T, a straight good-looking older dude, calls everyone "Daddy." Even chicks. Even his mom. Everyone's "Daddy" to T.

What an incredible trip! Best night of my life hands down. If you're going to start taking drugs, you might as well start with the good shit. Thank you, T. I'd ask you to marry me, but I think I'm in love with your friend. How the hell did I get together with *Keith* you ask? Last you heard I was rage-fucking Jonathan again. One night last month when Jonathan and I were at the Pig having coffee, Keith had just finished his shift and was sitting at a table near us talking to a co-worker. Every time I'd look in his direction, he was looking at me. All of a sudden, he got up and walked over to us.

"Hey, what's up?" he said, reaching out his hand. I reached mine up to meet his and we engaged in a vigorous handshake.

"Oh, you know," I replied, at a sudden loss for words. "Coffee."

"Hey, man," he said to Jonathan, reaching out his hand to shake his. A little surprised, Jonathan unfolded his arms so that he could shake Keith's hand.

"Hi."

Keith brought his attention back to me. "I was wondering if you'd like to see a show with me tomorrow night?" he asked, smooth as silk. He really is Spider-man.

"What kind of show?"

"The Beta Band at the Roxy."

"The *Beta* Band?" I said. "Never heard of 'em."

"I'm sorry to hear that. Then it's time."

"Oh yeah? It's time? Well in that case, sure. I'll go with you. Why the hell not? It's time." I glanced over at Jonathan, curious about his reaction. He was wearing his own poker face and appeared unfazed. "Here's my number," I said, scrambling to write it on the napkin I was using. I couldn't get my digits written fast enough. 818… "I'll see you tomorrow," I said, handing the napkin to him with trembling hand.

"Yes you will. The Beta Band at the Roxy," he repeated slowly. "Take it easy, man. Nice seeing you," he shook Jonathan's hand again before departing out the front door and into the hot summer night.

"Why the hell not, right? I said to Jonathan who offered little reaction. "It's the Beta Band at the Roxy after all."

"Sure. Why the hell not," he replied, oozing with sarcasm. His voice always gives it away. I'm sure he wasn't thrilled by what had just transpired, but I didn't care. Spidey was looking hot as hell. The following evening, I accompanied him to the Roxy on Sunset Boulevard to see The Beta Band play.

They just released *The Three EPs* and were on the U.S. leg of their world tour. I don't know who I fell more in love with that night—Keith or the incredible music. I haven't been that turned on by a UK band since Def Leppard released *Hysteria* in the summer of '87. I'd never heard anything like the Betas before and was instantly hooked. I was so aroused by the experience that when Keith brought me back to my apartment, we had sex. I had to. You don't get taken to see the Beta Band at the Roxy and not fuck the daylights out of the good soul who took you. That would be rude. That dreamy night was the beginning for us. About a month ago.

My blind eyes have been opened. My captive soul, freed. I am transformed. I swear, ecstasy made me fall in love with him. The "non-stop orgasm" that everybody at Palm Desert High School spoke of turned out to be the orgasm of love and empathy. We took our first hit around 2:00 a.m. and hung out in his tiny apartment talking, touching, kissing, and making the sweetest love.

As aroused as I was the entire time, I never came. I didn't want it to end and an orgasm would have ended it. I wanted him to merge with me forever. In between idyllic love making sessions we exchanged pudding-dipped strawberries between each other's mouths and caressed one another in places that'd never been touched. I still can't believe how beautiful it was. We could barely tear ourselves apart from one another.

Keith said that he loved me but admitted how "afraid" he was of "falling in love." All he kept saying was how "into" me he was. He sure seemed to mean it. In the midst of his confession, I filled my mouth with chocolate pudding so that he could suck it into his mouth. Then I put a plump strawberry in between my lips and he nibbled it down to the emerald green leaves.

Not long after I took the second hit, around 6:00 a.m., I thought I'd overdosed and was going to die. I was sitting on his couch drinking some orange juice when the volume was suddenly turned way up on my high. Not sure how else to describe it. It felt like whatever was going on in my body was suddenly amplified ten times, and I panicked. You would've, too. This intense rush of heat or emotion or sensation or whatever suddenly filled my body. I'd never taken drugs before. This was my first rodeo. Caffeine was the closest thing to a drug I'd ever consumed. I'd never even smoked weed, so I had no idea what the fuck was going on.

Terrified, I belly-flopped onto Keith's living room floor.

He rushed over to me and started rubbing my back. I immediately calmed down. It felt so good, his hands on my vulnerable bare skin. Gentle, good hands. My starved flesh barely recognized them. It'd been an eternity since I felt a gentle loving touch. He saved my life. Keith, my gentle prince, saved me from the fall.

I know the incident scared the shit out of him. I could see it in his frantic eyes once I was on the floor. He'd never done this drug before either. Only vicariously through T. We were virgins. We were the ecstatic blind leading the blind, and it was life-changing. He handled his panic brilliantly. Put his total focus on soothing me. Before I knew it, the panic turned to pure pleasure, and all I could do was moan, groan and thank him for saving me. I fell deeper in love with each caress his hands made over my naked back. Maybe I *had* died.

I was so impressed, so touched, so deeply moved. Saving my life notwithstanding, Keith let me talk about my mom for hours. He listened as I recounted her harrowing death six months earlier and what it did to me. I hadn't spoken about my grief in this way. I hadn't cried, nothing. It was an incredible release. A total purge. Long overdue. Ecstasy, like love itself, is a drug you never want to come off of.

The magical effects lingered into the next day. I couldn't tear myself away from my savior. We slept until about 7:00 p.m. then went to Eat Well for dinner followed by the Pig for free iced mochas. Everything tasted better. It was incredible. Life is incredible. Have I found the one? Is this why I had to lose Matthew? So that I could find Keith?

***

**Friday, February 18, 2000**

Dear Diary,

Oh my God, yesterday was awful. My emotions spun completely out of control. I was out of control inside. Pure chaos. A rotten feeling I know all too well. After Jonathan and I went into the Pig on Wednesday night, I was a complete basket case. It felt like a bomb had detonated inside of me. Nobody knows about these feelings but me; this unmitigated hell I go through inside. It can't even be articulated. It's too dreadful. Too overwhelming. You know how it feels when a massive wave slams you to the coastline, knocking the wind out of your lungs underwater? It's like that.

Only worse.

I don't know what I was expecting going in there, but the way Keith treated me was fucking hurtful. When I saw him, I called out his name to get his attention. He looked a bit startled but when he realized it was me, he stopped frothing somebody's milk and approached us. I gave him a hug and asked how he was doing.

"Great," he replied. Ouch. "How's acting?"

"*Acting?*" I said, beside myself.

"Your play."

"Oh. Uh, it's fine. It's great. How was your trip to Texas?"

"Man, I had a great time. Saw my folks and some other family I hadn't seen in a while. I even hung out at that bar T told us all about. Remember?"

"Sure," I replied, feigning to remember whilst shattering inside. After our excruciatingly impersonal exchange, Keith returned to his foam.

Jonathan and I ordered a round of iced mochas with croissants and grabbed a table as far from the espresso bar as possible. I tried to pull myself together, to present as alright. But I was merely "acting" the whole time.

A little while later I saw Keith looking at me as he walked over to his favorite spot behind the bar. I could barely gag down my iced mocha. What was otherwise a highly satisfying libation tasted like burnt death. When Keith's shift ended he came over to us and said goodbye. I felt ill. I was sure I'd puke up everything. The mocha, the pain au chocolat, my heart, everything. He didn't in any way, shape or form acknowledge anything that'd happened. He didn't in any way, shape or form appear distraught over our break up. A break up that he initiated out of the blue three weeks ago.

Nevertheless, I was kind to him. I wanted to strangle him but refrained. This feat, in spite of the emotional inferno that raged inside of me. I know now I can never step foot in that place again. I don't care how addicted to their espresso and ambiance I am. I'll choke down Starbucks on every other street corner in this wretched city if I have to.

My sweet, sweet Richard. Bless his precious gay heart. I hung out with him yesterday at the Horseshoe Café in Sherman Oaks. I was in bad shape. Dying yet again of another broken heart. I'm surprised it still beats considering the beating it's taken. As I sat on one of their couches trembling, my hot mocha clutched tightly between my knees, Richard sat next to me and caressed my back as I wept. They say, *"What cannot be said will be wept."* They were right.

"I had no idea you loved him this much."

"So much," I whimpered, taking a shaky sip of my coffee.

"I didn't realize you were *this* hurt."

"I'm inconsolable." Not even my drug of choice could do much to ease the horrific pain that engulfed every fiber of my being. My mother, God rest her tragic soul, used to tell me, "If there's a hell, this is it." I know what she meant now.

I've been so distraught over this break up that I called Pops, Diana, Billy, Blanche, and Sam—one after the other a few nights back—in search of solace that never came. Poor Billy's been forced to listen to me for hours upon hours. He doesn't seem to mind. He's been a good friend through all of this. The pain has been excruciating and talking to others about it is the only remedy though a fleeting one. When Matthew left two years ago I went into shock. Totally numb. I didn't even cry just like when my mom died. I ached in secret behind obligatory smiles. You don't cry when you're hit by a train. You absorb the impact and move on. This time around, that pain's a little harder to shake.

I just can't figure out what happened, what changed in Keith. It's been almost a month since the infamous Air concert at the Hollywood American Legion Hall. And it's been nearly three weeks since he broke up with me. I miss him so much; I want to jump out of my skin. Is this what heroin withdrawal feels like? Ironically, Keith used to compare breakups to drug withdrawal.

"You know it's like withdrawing off a drug, right? Love's a powerful drug. And when you get it, get it, get it and then suddenly you don't, you're going to hurt. You're going to want another hit."

What a premonition.

When I awoke at four o'clock yesterday morning the existential pain was at a fever pitch. My head throbbed. My whole body ached. My disjointed thoughts weaved and raced, and sleep was an unfaithful friend. I haven't suffered like this since that dreadful night in my Nissan Stanza when Matthew told me it was irretrievably over; that there was nothing I could do to salvage our tainted love even though I was fully prepared to do whatever it took.

How could Keith do this to me? How could he abandon me with no explanation at all? At least I knew why Matthew dumped me. I could count three or four or more reasons why. This time, I haven't a bloody clue. Everyone thinks he's too immature to handle a serious relationship. And that all the pot, ecstasy and computer shit are just a means of escape. My friends think he tries his best to avoid any real emotions.

Cynthia just called me here at work and said, "Destiny, now you know the truth. Don't give him another thought." Easier said than done.

She thinks people's feelings just change sometimes and that that's what happened here. She said that after he didn't respond to the letter I sent him she knew it was over. She said I just have to face the truth that for whatever reason Keith doesn't want to be with me.

I really hate him right now. I want to tell him how much I hate him and what a coward I think he is. Maybe I should. Email's the perfect way to do just that…

It's 10:38 a.m. I just sent him an email that read: "You know something, for a long time I thought you were the nicest guy I'd ever met. A veritable dream come true. And now that I really know you, I see that I was dead wrong. You're nothing but a pathetic coward."

Wow. I feel much better. After seven inseparable months, the guy breaks up with me over the phone while I'm at my dad's, telling me he doesn't love me. How fucking terrible is that? And now, he treats me as if none of it ever happened.

I'm tired of being hurt by men. What the fuck am I saying? *Boys.* Little boys. I had the time of my life with this guy. All that ecstasy we did. Sitting on the roof of his 1920s apartment building off Sunset all those late nights that made their way to dawn. Talking for hours about every last thing on our hearts. Listening to incredible music. Going to incredible shows. Walking around the city at night. Shit, we must've walked a hundred miles together. Full-body rubs for hours. The night we spent at Venice beach. Making the most tender love.

Sex with Keith was some of the best of my life. As bereft as I am right now there's no denying it. The ecstasy had a lot to do with it. I had incredible sex with Matthew, too. Stone cold sober sex. Not so much as a drop of vino ever stained our love making, and it was wonderful.

But drugs enhance physical pleasure exponentially as I would discover during my fleeting affair with Keith. They enhance the mental, emotional and spiritual side of things, too. This drug especially. Ecstasy dissolves barriers, eliminates hang ups, dismantles the ego and opens the heart to empathy. Shit, I even started to feel empathy for Linda the first night we took it. Stephen, not so much.

I can still see Keith's naked body, lean and smooth. I don't like big dudes, big muscles or hair in places it shouldn't be. I like lean, mean and clean. Skinny but not too skinny. Tall but not too tall. Which is why Keith is perfect. My physical ideal. The fact that he's got long hair doesn't hurt either. And of course, that exquisite cock. Not just nice. Not just big. Not just beautiful. Fucking exquisite. Throw a big dick in the mix and you're going to need rehab, therapy, stitches, all of it.

No wonder I'm so fucked up right now. I think what made sex so great with him was more than just his flawless physique and luscious equipment. What felt so good was the fact that when we did it, we were truly making love. The ecstasy bonded us quickly and deeply, infusing our sex with tantric flare. Having sex with him was literally a spiritual experience. I felt connected like never before. His heart and mine beat as one.

I hadn't felt any real feelings during sex since Matthew. You don't realize this shit until you've had some perspective. A little hindsight as it were. You never see the shit that's too close to you. Only once it's moved into your periphery does it become clear. I thought there were real feelings between Jonathan and I. Even crazy Stephen. But after seven months with Keith, I see that there weren't. It was just addiction. That cunning, baffling motherfucker.

Even though Keith and I fucked on the first date this detail didn't hinder our future sex. It only got better. Elders will tell you, "Don't fuck him on the first date. He'll lose respect and likely interest. You've got to keep that pussy a mystery for a while. Make 'em earn it." Well, not in this case. I'll never forget any of it. It was the happiest seven months of my life. After Matthew left, Keith restored my faith in love and good men. He had no idea all those things I told him that I did to Matthew were never, ever going to happen between us.

What makes this all so ironic is the fact that I treated Keith better than I *ever* treated Matthew. Not only did I never cheat, I never even considered it nor would I have ever considered it. I never hung up on him, not once. After losing Matthew I knew that I would never treat someone I loved that way again regardless of the inner war I waged. Yet, he's treating me as if I had. The irony is beyond dramatic.

I never wanted it to end. How could he want what we had together to end? How could he never want to be with me again? I wonder what it was about me that he couldn't handle. Was I too forthcoming about past relationship mistakes? The cheating on Matthew? Did I tell him too much too quickly? Is he pushing me away because he's afraid of something? Does he genuinely not have any feelings for me anymore like he said? Did he ever?

As Jonathan so adeptly put it, "It's the unanswered questions that haunt you."

***

**Monday, September 19, 1994**

To My Loveliest Destiny,

I can't tell you how wonderful it's been talking to you these past two days. It's almost like it's for the first time. All those times you hung up on me, and those days I went without talking to you were so very painful. I'd literally just sit and stare at the wall. I know they were painful for you. Probably more so. Painful for us both; I'll leave it at that.

When I think about you, I get so happy. I do feel pain because you're in New York, but I also feel so much joy knowing you're still with me. When I think of everything I've done and the fact that you're still with me and how lucky I am to have found a person like you, it gives me an overwhelming sense of joy. You're so beautiful, Destiny. You're such a wonderful person, full of so much life, goodness and love. If only you could see it as clearly as I do. And to think you're still with me considering that all of our problems have stemmed from me is the best feeling in the world.

When I think about what we've got over everyone else and our potential with this gift it blows my mind. I can't wait for my second chance with you starting December 22nd. Things will be different when you get back. I can't wait to show you. I'll finally be worthy of you. I'm so glad you liked the flowers. May they bring you joy and be a constant reminder of my endless love. These are going to be a grueling three months, but we'll pull through. Just concentrate on the matter at hand: being the best actress you can be.

I'm worried about you getting that abortion alone. Please try to have a friend there when it happens. I think it would make it a lot easier. For me anyway. This is a bad situation. I can't believe it had to happen again now. I think we're being tested for some reason. I mean really, could the first month have gotten any more difficult for us? How much more are we going to have to endure? I don't know, but we'll take it all in stride and move on. We've got what it takes—lots of love.

I wrote in one of my previous letters that this relationship needs to move to the next level. I feel like it's on my shoulders to make that happen. All you have to do is what you're doing now—stick with me. I think the second level involves us getting over our personal problems while we struggle through our lives in New York. That's going to be a task in itself let alone having to deal with all of my garbage. Our lives in New York are going to be wonderful. I think we're just going to have to pay our dues in our respective fields. That's what's happening with you right now. Just keep on truckin.'

Remember that I love you to the moon and back again.

Eternally yours,
Matthew Ian

***

*"One early writer says that the Grail was brought from heaven by the neutral angels. You see, during the war in heaven between God and Satan, between good and evil, some angelic hosts sided with Satan and some with God. The Grail was brought down through the middle by the neutral angels. It represents that spiritual path that is between pairs of opposites, between fear and desire, between good and evil. The theme of the Grail romance is that the land, the country, the whole territory of concern has*

*been laid waste. It is called a wasteland. And what is the nature of a wasteland? It is a land where everybody is living an inauthentic life, doing as other people do, doing as you're told, with no courage for your own life. That is the wasteland. And that is what T.S. Eliot meant in his poem The Waste Land." ©*

## Monday, February 28, 2000

Dear Diary,

This past weekend Jonathan and I escaped to San Francisco. We drove up Friday night when I got off work at Borders. It only took five hours to get there. We stayed at the Days Inn on Geary Street, got up Saturday morning and grabbed a coffee at this cool little cafe near the hotel. They made one of the best iced mochas I've ever had. I hadn't tasted an iced mocha that creamy and delicious since my early days at Espresso 2 a Tea with Matthew.

After coffee we walked to Fisherman's Wharf where we shared some chocolate confections, a prelude to fish and chips. The chocolate was yummy but the fish and chips sucked, another prelude of what was to come. From there we went to see a Georgia O'Keefe exhibit in the basement of the Palace of the Legion of Honor museum. But, much like the fish and chips, it sucked. Feeling defeated and depressed, we decided to go back to our hotel room and rest. I was exhausted from all the walking and sucking.

Upon waking from a short nap, Jonathan offered to give me a foot rub. I didn't really want him touching me, but it sounded nice and I figured my feet were the safest bet. Boy, was I wrong. Everything was fine until he molested my unsuspecting foot. That's right, he took my bare foot in a vulnerable moment and pressed it smack dab against the massive erection barely contained by his boxer shorts.

"What in the mother fuck are you doing motherfucker?" I hissed at him, jerking my foot away from his swollen shaft. Clutching my violated foot, I went numb. Tom and Cynthia were right. He did try to fuck me just as they'd so keenly predicted. As my poor foot reeled from the shock and trauma, I made it clear to him that I wasn't interested in having sex.

"I want to fuck you so bad, Destiny. Please fuck me," he whimpered, gazing down upon his cock which appeared to be vibrating. There's nothing I hate more than a whimpering man, slave to his dick, begging for pussy.

"You know how distraught I am over Keith. I can't bear the thought of having sex with someone right now." By that, I meant that I couldn't bear the thought of having sex with *him* right now. Or ever. "You were pretty distraught on your birthday over the fact that Linda was fucking Stephen, but you had sex with me then. I'm pretty sure you enjoyed it, too."

"Please," I snapped.

"In fact, I'm certain of it."

"Stop."

"I'll never forget that orgasm you had."

"Fucking stop."

"That pussy squeezed tighter than a vise grip."

"You're making me sick."

"Remember that orgasm? I sure do. I can still feel it."

"I've had lots of incredible orgasms in my life. Too many to recall. But that was then and this is now, and I am not interested."

"You're cruel."

"Hurt people hurt people."

"You don't know what you want."

"I know what I *don't* want."

"You were hurt on your birthday. Devastated as I recall. Your best friend betrayed and humiliated you. What's the difference now?"

"Keith is the difference now. Haven't you been paying any fucking attention? We spent a five-hour car ride yesterday unpacking the nuances of my excruciating pain."

"Please, the guy got you hooked on drugs."

"I love him. Madly."

"You told me the same damn thing."

"Well, I was mistaken."

"I'm sorry. It's just that…"

"What?"

"What changed, Destiny? I don't understand, and it's killing me. You used to love fucking me. You used to love *me*. At least you said you did. Don't you remember? It wasn't that long ago. Don't you remember the first time we made love?"

"I'm gonna puke."

"On the floor of my apartment while Matthew was at work."

"Shut the fuck up."

"You were so reluctant and the next thing I know, I'm pounding you into the floor and you're begging me to come inside you."

"You make me sick."

"Don't you remember that? Where did she go? Where'd that Destiny go? I miss her."

"That Destiny was not in her right mind. Can we not rehash all that shit right now? I'm not in the fucking mood. I'm beyond depressed and can't even think about it."

"I'm sorry. I'm hurting, too."

The truth of the matter is that I'm not attracted to Jonathan in the least. I was at one point but not anymore. It's the weirdest thing. We met while working together at Barnes & Noble in Northridge. I found him snobbish at first then slowly develop an attraction. It was something about his prominent Lebanese nose and the fact that he graduated from UCLA with a political science degree that turned me on. So, we have an affair behind Matthew's back. Being the last straw in a string of affairs, Matthew finally dumps me after four and a half tumultuous years. End of January 1998. And now, I'm completely disgusted by Jonathan. Literally overnight my once aching desire to do bad things with the guy is dead. Gone. It's like, when Matthew left, my attraction to Jonathan went with him. Never to return except by fluke.

Charles Bukowski wrote, *"Once a woman turns against you, forget it. They can love you, then something turns in them. They can watch you dying in a gutter, run over by a car, and they'll spit on you."* It's strange but true. I'm speaking from first-hand experience.

Following the disturbing foot molesting incident, we pulled ourselves together and drove to Berkeley. There, we found a dark dank depressing bar—the perfect backdrop to marinate in our mutual despair. There we were, the two of us, in equal agony over unrequited love. All I could think about was how much I wished Keith would've been sitting across from me instead of Jonathan.

My God, a year ago I was in Europe with Jonathan agonizing over Matthew. History's repeating itself. I was cruel to him on that trip, too. Not only did I not fuck him once, but I unleashed a protracted verbal assault on the poor guy unlike any I'd deployed before. "No one will ever want you," I told him over dark chocolate croissants and doppio espressos near the Louvre. "You're disgusting."

I should have been thrilled to be there. Instead, I was wretched. That picture he took of me in Pere Lachaise said it all. Black I.N.C. turtleneck under black Guess overalls shot in black and white against a sprawling gray necropolis. Indeed, my world was black as night on that trip. And here I am feeling the exact same way in the City by the Bay. What the fuck is my life?

Before we went to sleep he got weird on me again. Asked if there was ever a chance for us and wouldn't let up on it. Finally, I told him point blank, "No, there isn't." Just like Matthew had told me that night in my Nissan.

The next morning Jonathan and I drove to the Golden Gate Bridge. What a beautiful view of the city and Alcatraz. For a minute, I forgot how sad I was. The picturesque scene before me; the fresh hope I sensed beyond the iconic steel bridge were potent enough to induce a temporary amnesia. I forgot all about the wasteland that was my life. Desperate to keep the good mood going, I got one more iced mocha from my favorite new spot before departing to Davis to see Shannon, Jonathan's ex-girlfriend.

I think he had aspirations of rekindling a romance with her since it wasn't working out between us. Problem was, she was still with the cross-eyed boyfriend, although Jonathan believed Shannon and Steve had broken up. I told him not to go see her, but he wouldn't listen. Jonathan thought he was hiding his pain but it was glaring. During lunch, Shannon was talking about something or another, and when I looked at Jonathan across the table his eyes were glazed over and vacant. He looked ill, and I acutely felt the pain he was feeling. In a flash of empathy, I saw myself in him.

During our journey back to L.A. he described a heavy weight on his chest. I didn't realize how much this guy hangs onto things. He kept saying how he and Shannon were "right for each other," and how maybe there was "still a chance" since all this time had gone by. He'd deluded himself into believing they could return to the previous state of their relationship.

"You can't go back," I told him. "Don't you know that? You can't go back." Upon hearing my own words everything sort of slowed down. It was like, I was telling him but the message was actually for me. I felt my heart collapse a little deeper into my own chest. He doesn't get it yet. I've learned my lesson. All I need to do is recall my last conversation with Matthew when he said the following to me over the phone: "Destiny, you and I will *never* be together again. As far as being friends one day, I, I... I don't know..."

Ouch.

When Jonathan dropped me off at my apartment I genuinely felt sorry for him. The guy's anguish permeated the cabin our entire drive home. I felt sorry for him because I didn't want to hug him goodbye, and he knew it. Nevertheless, he drove around my building and called me from the front gate so that he could, as he put it, "give you a proper hug." It made me wholly uncomfortable.

To think that I lost the best thing that ever happened to me for someone I can't bear to be touched by is confounding. He's going back to Cincinnati on Wednesday. I probably won't see him for several months. Perhaps we really can't be friends.

\*\*\*

**Thursday, March 2, 2000**

Dear Diary,

I received an email from Jonathan this morning ending our friendship. I had a feeling he was going to do this. Honestly, it's for the best. I'm not upset. I wasn't sure if I could've continued having a "friendship" with him after the way he behaved in San Francisco. By the time we got back to L.A. I was more disgusted than ever. I wonder if he'll ever be happy, what with his insatiable neediness and all.

Now get this—Dominic from Triad Entertainment (my day job) came to see me when I got off work at the bookstore Tuesday night. Dominic is Jim Fauci's nephew from Chicago who assists him back in the audio department. He called the front desk that morning and asked me when we were going to "go out"? Without hesitation I told him "tonight" then remembered I was working.

"Oh shit. I'm working at Borders tonight. Never mind."

"You have another job?"

"I'm a receptionist by day and a book whore by night."

"And you're just my type. I'll come visit you when you get off then."

"I'll believe it when I see it." A few breaths later we hung up. Lo and behold, at 10:30 p.m. he called me at the bookstore from Johnny's place. Johnny's my boss and the office manager at Triad. He's also one of

Dominic's best friends. When he called I happened to be at the info desk and answered. "Thank you for calling Borders Books & Music in Canoga Park. This is Destiny. How can I help you?"

"Hey gorgeous, it's Dom." It took me a second to ascertain who the fuck "Dom" was.

"Well, well, well."

"What are you doing?"

"Selling books. What are you doing?"

"Hanging out with Johnny P."

"Hi, Johnny P."

"Destiny says hello," I heard him say. "You're just a working girl, ain't you?"

"The bills ain't going to pay themselves."

"What kind of ice cream should I bring you?"

"You're actually coming to see me?"

"I am."

"Rocky road, of course."

"Alrighty, gorgeous. Rocky road it is. I'll see you soon." We hung up. At the stroke of midnight there he was, waiting for me in the Borders parking lot.

"What in the hell are you doing here?" I asked him.

"I'm here to see you."

Curiously, there was no ice cream anywhere to be found.

"Where's the rocky road you got my hopes up for?"

"Oh man, I couldn't find any after I left JP's."

"Lyin' bastard."

"Let me make it up to you and buy you a drink." Unable to turn down a free drink of any kind, I suggested that we go to TGI Friday's. It was up the street a few blocks on Canoga near Ventura Blvd. We sat at one of the red and white striped high-top tables above the bar and ordered a pair of strawberry margaritas. As we sipped he proceeded to tell me that he wanted to hang out with me more outside of work.

"You mean you want to fuck me."

"That, too."

I didn't mind. I always thought he was sexy in a weird sort of way. So, he came back to my apartment and we fooled around all night. Although we didn't have sex, we did almost everything else including him going down on me for quite some time. He seemed to enjoy it. *A lot.* I had no idea he possessed such a lustful appetite for me. We were all over the place. On my bed, the floor, back up on the bed. At one point he was naked and I had a little white t-shirt on, and he was trying hard to put it in, but I wouldn't let him.

"Fuck me," he kept saying, slobbering everywhere. "Please fuck me." But I wouldn't. Eventually, he fell asleep. Surreal. You just never know, do you? Then last night he called wanting to get together again, but I told him I was getting coffee with my friend David. Ain't it funny how when something else comes along you start to forget about the person you were with before? What's that saying: *The only way to get over somebody is to get under somebody else.* I was so bummed about Keith. Dare I say *shattered.* And now, I hardly think about him.

Honestly, I'd like to have a lover and not a boyfriend. Someone to come over and fuck me and that's it. No muss, no fuss. I spend most of my time with my friends, investing my energy in those relationships and keep my lover/lovers on the side. Like bacon. Am I delusional? Perhaps. Is this using men for their penises? Definitely. Does this make me a terrible woman? Who gives a fuck!

The bottom line is, I'm going to be very cautious from here on out with regard to who I get close to. I have to find a way to be involved but keep my distance. I can't fall in love with just anyone. For a while at least. I need to learn how to be comfortable being single and/or just dating. Someone like Dominic's perfect because you know you can't take him seriously; that he is, always has been, and can never be anything other than a charming idiot.

About Jonathan. I'm kind of glad that's over. I see now that this whole time, even throughout Stephen and Keith, he was holding on to the hope that we'd have something again someday. At that bar in Berkeley he told me how troubled he is about love. He said he's been depressed for five years. Since Shannon broke up with him. Then what I did and now Noelle breaking up with him.

He said he's resolved it in his mind that there's something about him that women ultimately don't like. I liked him before I really knew him. Not to mention the fact that he's the reason Matthew left me. And when I told him that I'd cheated on Matthew with Curtis prior to cheating with him, that seemed to bother him, too. He said he always thought he and I had something special while engaged in our affair, but now sees that it wasn't special at all.

"It was a pattern."

My conversation with David last night was enlightening as ever. I enjoy our talks immensely. He's a psych major at Pierce College and a regular at the bookstore. We've kindled a friendship the past few months since he's in the store almost every day. He thinks my mistake was telling Keith every dirty detail about my cheating past, and that when he saw how friendly I was to the guys from Triad at the Air concert it only fueled his paranoia.

How do you convince someone that who you were in the past needn't be a barometer for who you are now or will be in the future? I realize it's a tough sell. When Matthew finally left and I realized he wasn't coming back, I had an epiphany. A moment of stark clarity. I knew that never again would I take someone I loved—who loved me back and treated me well—for granted. I would never cheat on anyone that I was in a serious relationship with again, and I haven't. It's a goddamn tragedy I had to learn this lesson in the costliest way.

Maybe that's the only way some of us learn.

Ever my analyst, David suggested that I not mention my romantic past to the next guy I'm with. "Just tell 'em you were studying to become a nun in your youth then had a spiritual awakening. Yeah, tell him that."

*   *   *

**Tuesday, September 20, 1994**

Destiny, My Love,

I decided to take time out from studying for my government test to write you a letter. It's almost 3:30 p.m. your time. I wonder what you're doing. Every time I look at my framed pictures of you, I have to take a second to stare. You're so beautiful. I miss you so much. I can't wait for these three months to be over. Now, please! I hope everything is going well with school. You decided not to try and transfer studios. That's okay. I think when things normalize you'll begin to enjoy the Practical Aesthetics Workshop more. David Mamet's an amazing writer and William H. Macy's an amazing actor. You're in good hands.

I feel awful about the abortion on Saturday. I'm going to see your parents that day. It'll be strange. When I'm finishing my paper route that morning you'll be making your way to the clinic. By the time I wake up it should be all over. Then I'll have to wait five hours to see how you're doing. I'm happy Vashia's going with you. That makes me feel a lot better. I wish I could be there. I feel like I'm ducking responsibility for all this by sending you money and hoping for the best. I feel so helpless. It feels like I can't do anything but patiently wait. You've seemed more at ease with it lately except for being so sick. I hope you felt better today. I sure hope this decision is the right one, and that we can focus on looking forward to our reunion on December 22ⁿᵈ.

My father went to the therapist yesterday and said it went well. I have to wait until he's finished to see the guy. I asked my dad how many more times he thinks he'll go, and he said four. Hopefully I only have to wait a couple of weeks. I want to get this show on the road. I'm going to get to the bottom of my problem. Things will be different when you return, Destiny. I can't wait to show you. I can see myself changing. I'm seeing things about the relationship in a way I didn't before. It all just makes more sense now as to why we've been having all these problems. And I realize that I'm the center of it all.

The first hurdle we're going to get over is my better understanding of what's been going on inside me far too long. The second is for you to forgive me so that we can put all this behind us. Living together in New York is going to be difficult enough without all this creeping in. You said a lot of good things in the letters you sent me. You *are* my "one and only." Never doubt that. I just think that I have something in my psyche that hasn't caught up with the present time. It's nothing catastrophic, but I need to better understand it. I can't believe how loving and patient you've been.

After eleven months of me torturing you with all of this, I wonder how I got so lucky to have you fall in love with me. I'm the luckiest man alive. I'm going to show you that I truly feel that way. You're going to have to start getting used to things being different, the way they should've been. I'm warning you. Start preparing for it.

You did say one thing in the first letter that caught my eye, because I'm a jealous boyfriend. You said that you've been hanging around with guys, "many of them appealing." This caught me off guard. I don't know if you said it to hurt my feelings or if it's true. It just hit me as strange because you've never talked that way before. I've also sensed a couple of times on the phone that when you told me you hung out with people, you weren't comfortable telling me that there were guys there. I'm assuming you meant PAW people and friends of your roommates. I don't know why I decided to get on this tangent. It's just that the sound of "appealing" and "guys" in the same sentence made my stomach drop. Now I realize how all my shit must've made you feel. I'm a little more empathetic than you give me credit for.

I told your dad yesterday that the more I talk to you, the more I miss you. He laughed. It's strange though. The more I talk to you on the phone, the more I need to talk to you the next day and the day after. It's really strange. Talking makes me crave you more.

Something I realized yesterday and think you should do more often is write me letters. You write so beautifully. But you've only sent four since I left you on the curb in New York. It always picks me up to write to you. You've been sick, I realize that, but I think it would help. Just tell me everything that happened to you that day and whatever else comes to mind. There's nothing in the world better than reading a letter from the one you love.

I saw Jamie and Ron last night. I shouldn't have gone out to the compound, but I did. We watched *The Sheltering Sky*. That's the last time I do that on a school night. Ron asked how you were doing. I also talked to Nick on Sunday night. He didn't ask about you. I know that pisses you off. Don't let it. Nick would love to ask me about you. He's just not able to deal with himself and whatever residual feelings he has for you.

The more I think about the whole Rick thing, the stranger it all seems to me. I'm probably just going off on a jealous boyfriend trip again but hear me out. This guy's supposedly my friend. I realized at this very moment that he's never asked me about you. Which strengthens my theory about those two (Nick and Rick) not feeling comfortable when I utter the exquisite name "Destiny." Rick can't talk with me about my girlfriend of almost a year but is writing letters to you in New York with an intent I won't begin to get into, asking you not to tell me because he allegedly asks that of all his correspondences. Do you think when he writes to Pat in Austin he says, "Don't tell anyone what I've told you"? Bullshit.

Rick's in love with you. How's all this supposed to make me feel? Am I ever supposed to feel comfortable around this guy? I feel like he's a vulture circling above waiting for us to end so that he can glide down and mop up. I know that I have nothing to worry about on your end, but it's *my* end that I wonder about. Do you think I should talk with him about all this? I like Rick and value his friendship, but on one level I look at all this and say *fuck it*.

I can't believe it's been a year since we went up the mountain, took that walk, confessed our mutual attraction, you got the role in *Not Now, Darling,* and we all moved into that shitty house in Indio. It boggles my mind. It's amazing how time flies when you're in love. We talked about this the other night, but the more I think about it the more I'm amazed. Wow! It's been a beautiful year. And the next one is going to be even better. Wait and see. I've been writing this letter for over an hour now, so I must be going. I love you. Write me a letter back as soon as you finish reading this one. Always think: *Matthew loves me.*

Your best friend forever,
Matthew Ian

***

*"When people get married because they think it's a long-time love affair, they'll be divorced very soon, because all love affairs end in disappointment. But marriage is a recognition of a spiritual identity. If we live a proper life, if our minds are on the right qualities in regarding the person of the opposite sex, we will find our proper male or female counterpart. But if we are distracted by certain sensuous interests, we'll marry the wrong person. By marrying the right person, we reconstruct the image of the incarnate God, and that's what marriage is." ©*

**Friday, March 10, 2000**

Dear Diary,

STOP THE INSANITY! Last evening, I accompanied Dominic to the art exhibit of one of his hipster friends in downtown L.A. Let's just say the evening didn't go too well. The guy's a fucking maniac. Shit started rolling downhill around the time we left his place on our way to Adam Brown's.

As I was getting into his car with iced mocha in hand, Dominic smacked my ass unreasonably hard causing it to fly all over me. Whipped cream literally hung from my nose. His startling gesture hurt like hell and made me so mad, I had no other choice but to flip the bitch switch. You don't ruin a perfectly fine iced mocha of mine for bullshit and get away with it. What's worse, he didn't even offer to replace it.

Within thirty seconds at this exhibit I wanted to jump out of my skin. That place and those people were not my scene. Dom started shootin' the shit with some dudes he knew as I made my way inside to check out the art. Not impressed. After ten minutes of staring blankly at dismal walls, I found Dominic and asked him for the keys to his car. I wanted to lie down and plot my swift escape. A familiar voice inside my head kept screaming, "Wrong! Wrong! Wrong!"

I fumed in his car for twenty minutes before dude finally returned. When he did, I wasted no time telling him that I don't want to continue seeing him. "This isn't working for me," I said.

"Are you serious?"

He was genuinely shocked.

"As a heart attack." Feeling guilty all of a sudden like a true codependent, I reined it in a bit. "It's not you. It's me."

"Obviously."

"It's just that…I shouldn't be getting involved with someone right now. I'm not over my ex. You know this."

Dominic was less than thrilled with my admission and couldn't understand why I'd want it to end. "Don't you even want to give it a chance?"

"No."

"Just yesterday you said how great we get along."

"I was optimistic yesterday."

"What happened in 24 hours?"

"You spilled my coffee."

"You know what," he snapped all indignant-like, "call me in a couple months when you're ready. I'll buy you a coffee." By this point the guy's wasted. I mean, like shit-faced from all the liquor and weed. All I wanted to do was get back to Northridge. Fortunately, he let me drive his car home while he went with some dude from the exhibit off to God-knows-where. That poor guy. He was annoyed with Dom too because he kept calling him "Fucko" and "Motherfucker" all night.

It's amazing how drugs and alcohol can reveal a person's true nature for good or ill. I swear, this cat reminds me so much of Stephen it's uncanny. The way he guzzles booze and how it makes him act is virtually identical. And like Stephen, when he's sober, Dominic's fine. Dare I say, semi-fun. But when he starts drinking, forget it. All hell breaks loose. I remember Rick Saloomey from Triad telling me about the time Dominic showed up to a paintball game high on acid. Rick made it clear that Dom could get quite obnoxious.

I should have listened.

Today he's acting like I didn't mean what I said about not wanting to see him anymore. He called me this morning looking for his car keys and asked, "Do you really not want to see me anymore?"

Derek and Danny McBride were standing in reception, so all I said to him was, "We'll talk about it."

Now he's here in the office. He keeps coming over and kissing me on the head, acting as if nothing's wrong. What's this guy's problem? Ever since he came to see me at Borders he's wanted to spend every goddamn night with me. Under the spell of the magic pussy, I suppose. I spent last weekend with him and his Chicago Italian family. Saturday morning—breakfast at the Marriott. Saturday night—dinner at Lawry's in Beverly Hills. Nicest restaurant I've ever been to. Since that first night he's treated me like his girlfriend. He even introduced me to Tommy Lee at Yankee Doodles three nights ago.

We were sitting at the bar in the restaurant having drinks. I'd just gotten off work from Borders and had also worked eight hours at Triad. I'm exhausted. All of a sudden it looks as though Dom sees somebody he knows behind me.

"I'll be right back," he said, scurrying away. I didn't see who it was that he saw. Fifteen minutes later, my tired ass is still sitting on that barstool waiting for him to return. Five minutes after that I slurped down the rest of my margarita and went looking for him. In a separate dining room, I see him standing in group of people. I make a feverish beeline toward him, furious. "What the fuck?" I snapped, charging into the group.

"Destiny, meet Tommy Lee," he said. As if they were long-lost buds.

"Hi there, how ya doin'?" I said, shaking his hand vigorously then immediately bringing my attention back to the douchebag who ditched me at the bar. "Can we get the fuck out of here? I worked two jobs today, I'm fucking tired." With that, Tommy Lee and his entourage bolted like a flock of seagulls stage left. Apparently, they'd had enough of Dominic too and seized the opportunity I provided to bounce.

The bottom line is Dominic's an alcoholic and I can't get involved. We've had sex a few times and it's alright, but it's certainly not worth the insanity. Last night on the way to the exhibit he said, whilst I was in my terrible mood, "Deep down you love me. You love me." We've been hanging out for a week, and I love him? Perhaps it's he who's doing the loving and a little projecting. Shit, if I do love him, it's so deep as to not even register on a conscious level.

I had the best time Tuesday night yakking about the whole fiasco with David and TJ at the info desk at Borders. TJ's my highly sexed ex-military coworker who doesn't discriminate. He'll fuck 'em if they're old, young, fat, ugly. He don't give a damn. He's a self-described "equal opportunity lover." A fucking scream. When he, David and I chat, it's always an adventure.

David thinks I have a potential stalker on my hands. He believes Dominic fell in love with me after we had sex and now sees me as some sort of long-term girlfriend material. TJ, conversely, doesn't know what to make of Dominic's antics. They both agreed he purposely acted flirty with me at the Air concert in order to upset Keith. It worked. Thanks a lot, Fucko.

74

Honestly, I don't want to get involved with him. Especially after last night. Maybe I'll keep him around for sex but absolutely nothing else. I'm just going to keep telling him that I'm not ready to get involved right now. That my boyfriend (Keith), whom I deeply love, broke up with me not long ago and it's best if I heal that cavernous wound before embarking on another relationship. After all, what you don't heal in your singleness will spread like a virus in your togetherness.

It was so funny, after we left the bullshit art thing and I told him I didn't want to see him anymore, Dominic blurted out, "Maybe you need a Geisinger" to which I swiftly replied, "Yeah, maybe. Dorky Canadian accountants really get me wet." Geisinger is one of the accounts at Triad. Super nice guy. Speaks fluent French. Dominic also said something like, "Sorry, but I won't be another one of your pushover boyfriends."

Okay then, will you at least be a sane one?

***

**Tuesday, March 28, 2000**

Dear Diary,

I'm so thrilled. Johnny's hooking me up with two hits of ecstasy tomorrow. At last! He said it's the best. Powder form, pure as fuck. I haven't taken any ecstasy since the infamous Air concert in January with Keith, so I'm ecstatic. How lucky am I to have a boss that hooks me up with the primo shit? As always, I'm writing this from my windowless post at the Triad reception desk.

I spent the entire weekend with Dominic. On Saturday we hung out with Richard all day. Picked him up around one o'clock and took him to Pane Dolce for lunch. I had a fragrant green salad, a quad shot non-fat iced cappuccino with cinnamon dust and two chocolate-dipped Madeleines. The perfect pairing. Bitter and sweet.

Afterwards, we perused a music store near the Horseshoe. I couldn't resist purchasing albums from Supreme Beings of Leisure, Hooverphonic, Air, and The Verve. From there we hit Babies R Us. No, not for me! We had to get baby shower gifts for Bret Michaels of Poison. Dominic asked me to accompany him to Bret's baby shower this weekend. His cousin Jim is good friends with the band and engineered several of their albums including *Look What the Cat Dragged In*. The Faucis are considered family.

After Ventura Blvd. we ended up at Johnny's place for Bailey's, whippets and weed. Can you imagine! We sat around smoking weed and inhaling whippets at the boss's pad. Only in L.A. Well, I didn't smoke anything. That's Johnny and Dominic's thing. I did my thing—drank Bailey's and made Richard do a whippet before I would. It was no biggie and I needn't do it again. Nothing compares to ecstasy.

Or coffee.

After that we all went back to Woodland Hills and got in Dominic's jacuzzi. Me, my boss, a spoiled Italian fuckboy and my gay best friend all in a jacuzzi together. I was the sole chick in a swirling pool of dick. Unfortunately, all the weed he smoked made Richard a little loopy and he decided it was best if he went home. He admitted yesterday what was really fuckin' with him, and it wasn't the pot. It was the fact that he was hoping to engage in a threesome with Dominic and I that never materialized.

*Huh?*

That took be back, made me uncomfortable, so I played dumb. I love Richard with all my heart, but I'll never engage in a threesome, twosome or any other sex act with him. He's like my brother from another mother who happens to appreciate wiener as much as I do.

After driving Richard home Dominic and I shared a fajita burrito at Jerry's Deli in Woodland Hills. I sat there listening to him drone on and on about how "crazy" he allegedly is about me. He wouldn't shut up about it. The more beer he drank, the more he driveled on.

"I'm in love with you, Destiny. Always have been," he said as gooey balls of salsa-infused cheddar rolled down his chin.

"Always?" I asked, unable to conceal my skepticism. "We just met."

"Some things you just know."

"You're in love with my buttermilk biscuit. That's what I know."

"She's nice, too. So warm and friendly."

We shared a laugh.

Although it was difficult for me to fathom his eternal love, it was still nice to hear. We women enjoy and appreciate hearing certain pleasant things like: "You're so lovely," and "You have beautiful eyes," and "Your pussy feels so good." Conversely, there are things we definitely don't enjoy hearing come from the mouths of our lovers. For me, certain careless admissions by those I was dating had a devastating effect on both my psyche and the ultimate fate of the union. For the more sensitive souls among us words are like weapons, sharper than knives when wielded without thought or empathy.

Take my beloved Matthew for example. When he said to me early on in our relationship, *"Do you know how I know that I love you? Because you're not the kind of girl I'd look twice at on the street, but I still love you,"* that was the beginning of our eventual end. I could never shake it. I was *not* the kind of girl he'd look twice at on the street. And he could never explain exactly what he meant. This haunted my younger more vulnerable self to the point of total destruction.

But I digress...

After Jerry's, Dominic and I ended up at BJ's where the drinking and driveling continued. He whined about how he didn't think that I liked him the way he liked me. I did my best to reassure him that I liked him plenty, even going so far as to utter the unthinkable: "I love you, Dominic." The moment the words spattered out of my mouth, I wondered if they were true or if I said it to shut him up. All I know is that yet again the booze transformed him into an obnoxious fool.

Back at his place he got a little too rough in the sack and it really bothered me. What he doesn't realize is that I've already been roughed up by a crazy man or two. I wasn't going to put up with it again. I went to sleep royally pissed off. And you want to know the main reason why I was so pissed? It wasn't because he fucked me too hard with that misshapen thing. It was because after the fucking surceased, dude kept blasting *Strangelove Addiction* by Supreme Beings of Leisure on my boombox, and I couldn't sleep.

When I awoke from my nightmare Sunday morning, he had a huge cup of fresh-squeezed orange juice from Jamba and a long-stem red rose waiting for me on the floor outside his bedroom. Realizing he went too far the night before, Dominic took me to the Coffee Bean on Reseda knowing that would likely cheer me up. It did. Coffee always cheers me up. It's my anti-depressant of choice and always has been since I first got hooked on those Gloria Jean's frothy iced cappuccinos at the Palm Desert Town Center back when I was with Phil. Shortly before I left him to be with Matthew.

"Here's that coffee I owe you," Dominic said, handing me a large ice blended mocha with whip.

"It's about time."

From there it was off to Bret Michael's house nestled somewhere in the California desert near Magic Mountain. Thank God Jim, Janine and their friend Tracy were there or I'd have felt like a jerk. Dominic was all over the place. A righteous lunatic. If ever someone was the "life of the party," it's this clown. From our first steps inside Bret's sprawling Santa Fe style house Dominic was "on."

Within ten minutes I'd met all the members of Poison: Bret Michaels (lead vocals), Rikki Rockett (percussion), Bobby Dall (bass) and C. C. DeVille (guitar). Bobby Blotzer, the drummer for Ratt, was also there. What a surreal day. I got to hang out with a band that defined my adolescence. A time that feels more like myth than memory to me now. Before I ever fell in love with Def Leppard, I was in love with Poison.

As I write this, I'm flashing back to 14. I'd just moved to the desert to live with my mom and was thrilled to be reunited with her. I'd been living with old man Jones up until this point. Kay spent most of my childhood loaded on pills, scrapping with my dad, couch surfing, homeless, in the hospital or rehab. Although Pops had been physically abusive, he was always there. He provided stability. I couldn't say the same thing about my poor mom. But when I turned 14 she'd just gotten sober and seemed to be doing well for the first time in my life. I desperately yearned for a relationship with her. Still do.

Kay and I were cramped but happy in her studio apartment off San Pablo and Highway 111 in Palm Desert. *The Esquire*. It was the summer of '87. *Dirty Dancing* had just been released, and I'd just gotten my period. I'll never forget what Kay said to me as my first blood ran down my inner thigh that afternoon in the bathroom.

"Just remember," she said, firing up another Winston, "you can get pregnant now." That was it. That's all she said to me on this momentous day. Not a single word was offered about how I might comport myself now that I was fertile.

One sweltering July day shortly thereafter, I'm at the ABC Club flaunting my new tunes. Mom had just bought me a brand-new cassette tape at Gemco: *Look What the Cat Dragged In* by Poison. I was ecstatic to have acquired a copy. I fell in love with the androgynous hair band thanks to MTV and our local 93.7 KCLB F.M. who played their songs religiously. When I showed the tape to a resident at the ABC Club—a drug and alcohol treatment center off Indio Boulevard where Kay had been a resident—the guy's classic response still echoes in my mind: "Dude, I'm in love."

That made two of us.

But I digress…

At one point during the baby shower I found myself seated atop a picnic bench in Bret's backyard. Before I could wrap my mind around where I was, bassist Bobby Dall came over and sat perilously close to me at my right. We had a wonderful conversation about how much we loved the desert and how it has its own unique, magical energy. I got the distinct feeling that he liked me. I'm sure I could've slipped him my number if still I behaved that way. But I don't, so I didn't.

After an hour or so the band broke out in an impromptu mini-concert that included performances of *Talk Dirty to Me*, *Unskinny Bop*, *Your Mama Don't Dance* and my favorite: *Fallen Angel*.

*Win big, mama's fallen angel*
*Lose big, living out her lies*
*Wants it all, mama's fallen angel*
*Lose it all, rolling the dice of her life*

*Now, she found herself in the fast lane*
*Livin' day to day*
*Turned her back on her best friends, yeah*
*And let her family slip away*

*Just like a lost soul caught up in a Hollywood scene*
*All the parties and the limousines*
*Such a good actress hiding all her pain*
*Trading her memories for fortune and fame* ©

I wanted so badly to jump off that picnic bench and dirty dance to the songs that defined my youth. But I didn't.

As I sat next to Jim and Janine's friend Tracy, a chick I met shortly after arriving, the strangest thing occurred. Now mind you, a lot of shocking things have been uttered to me over my 26 years, but this was something new. As we sat briefly alone on the bench this chick turned, looked me dead in the eye and said, "You know…I sucked Bret Michaels's cock. And I suck a mean cock," her nostrils, fully flared.

Not sure how to respond, I said the first thing that came to mind: "I believe that." And I meant it. Nostrils do not flare in that manner if a bitch ain't serious. Her pronouncement felt like a veiled threat, as if she were really saying—*Don't get any dick-sucking ideas, sister*. Little did she know, but I had zero intentions of sucking any dicks in the vicinity. I never even sucked Dominic's.

The most intriguing conversation of all occurred when someone, C.C. DeVille I believe, asked Dominic if I was his wife.

"Not yet," was his reply.

In spite of my crippling social anxiety and deep feelings of insecurity, I ended up having a pretty good time. All that white zinfandel probably had something to do with it. I'm not typically a white wine drinker but if that's my only option, I'll make it work.

After the baby shower Dominic and I went to the Cheesecake Factory in Woodland Hills for dinner. I ordered what Billy had the time we went there with his dad and Keith: Grilled salmon with garlic mashed potatoes, asparagus and a doppio espresso to wash it down. Dominic and I ended up staying the night at my apartment, but he started blaring Supreme Beings of Leisure again, and I couldn't sleep. This time, *Truth from Fiction*.

*I said: pretty one listen to me*
*Truth is all that's asked for*
*And love is steering you to the inevitable*
*But you can't stop trying*
*Or you may start crying*

*I can't tell truth from fiction*
*I can't tell truth from fiction©*

He conned me into spending the night with him again last night, too. I got there around 11:30 p.m. and we rolled around on his living room floor laughing before going to bed. Although I shouldn't get in the habit of it, I let him come inside me again. At first he wouldn't do it, but I guess he doesn't care anymore. I'd better get my ass on the pill or else I'll have a little Italian demon fetus growing inside me.

Speaking of which, Saturday night he told me that he wished we were shopping for our baby when we went to Babies R Us with Richard. Is this for real? I actually believed him. He's just so damn sweet and charming.

I'm at Triad right now and just went with him downstairs so he could smoke. He invited me to some party for *G vs. E* on Thursday night. We also discussed our little ecstasy excursion on Saturday. I suggested that we get a room at Venice beach. We can walk up and down the boardwalk to the Santa Monica pier, maybe ride the Ferris wheel and eat some Pop Rocks. We can start off the day with some fresh squeezed orange juice to enhance the drug and make our way down there early afternoon. If there's no alcohol involved, only ecstasy, I bet we'd have a blast.

He said something interesting to me just now when we were downstairs. He asked if we could leave the pier if we started to freak out. "What do you mean 'freak out'?" I asked him. "From the people? We can just go down to the beach to get away from them if need be." He seemed reluctant. It might have something to do with the comment he made on Saturday about not wanting to supply me drugs because then that's all I'll want from him.

Not entirely true.

Okay, so Mickey just asked me when I wanted to do ecstasy with *him*. I forgot we'd discussed it a while back. I didn't know what to say, so I played dumb. I think he has other activities in mind—SEX! If we could take it and hang out, talk, walk, etc., that would be fine but I doubt it's that simple. Especially after that comment he made about kissing me last week when we walked to Starbucks on our lunch break.

\*\*\*

**Friday, September 23, 1994**

To My Love, Destiny,

I just got off the phone with you. I called back three times. Once the line was busy, once you hung up, and the third time you wouldn't answer. I know all of this is hard for you. It's difficult for me, too. It's not fair to either one of us that you have to go to that clinic tomorrow, but hanging up on me doesn't help.

I know that I hurt your feelings when I told you that you'd upset me, but look at it from my perspective. I feel like you rarely do. Why can't you just talk to me? Why do you have to talk to Nick and Rick? Of all people, *those* two. I know you haven't anyone to talk to. But if you're going to call long distance, why not call me? I'm the one who loves you. What's so great about Nick that it hurts you that he doesn't call you? This shit's hard on me, too. Especially when you hang up on me.

I can't tell you how much I'm hurting and have been since all this started. Do you think Nick or Rick would go through what I have in this relationship? Do you think they could be as strong and loving as I've been and am? I know that for a split second I got angry and selfishly said something that hurt your feelings. I didn't mean to. Just look at it from my perspective for once.

Destiny, I'm behind you 100%. You know that. It's not fair to hang up on me. I'm scared, worried and confused about all of this. We've both been under a lot of stress lately. Let's not do this to one another. I realize that you're all alone back there. I'm the one you should be reaching out to not them. Can they do something for you that I can't? You said Nick was of no help. He's never been. When are you going to acknowledge and accept this? That's one reason why I got so upset. You should've called me.

God, I love you. If you think all of this is hard on you, try being me and having the person you love more than life itself *hang up on you again* 2,500 miles away. I know all of this is hurting you too, and I'll keep going through it until the day we die. It's just difficult to sit here waiting for your return call or wondering when it is that I'm going to get to talk to you again. These past six days that we've been talking have been wonderful. I've cherished every minute of our conversations. I'm praying to God that we can keep it like that until December 22nd.

I know that for a minute I was being insensitive to your feelings and your position in all of this. I'm so sorry for hurting you. It's just that you were obviously in a bad mood when you answered the phone. It sounded like you didn't even want to talk. You had that flippant "whatever" attitude that caught me off guard. Then the first thing you say is that you told Nick you're pregnant and that Rick was going to call you back. That caught me off guard too and hurt my feelings deeply.

Can you understand why it makes me uncomfortable to know that you're sharing the most sensitive topics of our relationship with two people that obviously have feelings for you and can't deal with me on a one-on-one level because of it? It hurts me to think that you called them to talk about our predicament when you could've called me. Maybe you did. I didn't see a message on the machine.

This is *our* life, *our* plight. They have no business knowing any of it. That was the problem last October. Everyone whose business it wasn't knew every detail of what was occurring in your, Phil's and my life. Now it's happening again. We told Nick about the miscarriage last winter. Now he knows about this. I've gone to Nick about our relationship problems myself. We shouldn't do that. That's why this time around I went to your father. You can talk to your parents. Your mom's always home.

I'll give you a call the second I receive any message from you. Darling, the reason all hurts is because we love each other so goddamn much. Don't push me away. It hurts us both too much. I've called twice more since beginning this letter.

Your love,
Matthew Ian

***

*"It's a very mysterious thing, that electric thing that happens, and then the agony can follow. The troubadours celebrate the agony of the love, the sickness the doctors cannot cure, the wounds that can be healed only by the weapon that delivered the wound. The wound is the wound of my passion and the agony of my love for this creature. The only one who can heal me is the one who delivered the blow. That's a motif that appears in symbolic form in many medieval stories of the lance that delivers a wound. It is only when that lance can touch the wound again that the wound can be healed."* ©

**Wednesday, April 5, 2000**

Dear Diary,

Dominic and I had the best weekend. Got to Santa Monica at about two o'clock on Saturday and checked into the Ocean Lodge. Once settled, we swallowed one of our pills and went out exploring. The weather was incredible. Balmy with a gentle breeze. Half an hour later we started to feel something.

It was mild.

We walked from the Santa Monica pier along the boardwalk all the way to Venice and back. We stopped in this funky little store where I sampled some incense. Dominic was sweet enough to buy it for me only to lose it shortly thereafter. From there, we sat on the beach and watched the blowing sand create this weird optical illusion. A sailboat in the distance looked like it was floating on the sand. Everything felt like a dream.

At the end of our walking tour of Venice, back in the little gift bazaar, we both flipped out when we saw pictures of the New York and Los Angeles skylines that had little blinking lights on them. We thought our eyes were playing tricks on us. After this we made our way back to our motel room where we decided to take the remaining pills. I took a long hot shower then got dressed. After a while I started feeling good. I mean, *really* good. So good that I bounced up and down on the bed to the Beatles' *Sergeant Pepper* in my black turtleneck and those green nylon pants.

*It was twenty years ago today*
*Sergeant Pepper taught the band to play,*
*They've been going in and out of style,*
*But they're guaranteed to raise the smile,*
*So may I introduce to you,*
*The act you've known for all these years,*
*Sergeant Pepper's Lonely Hearts Club Band.* ©

After a little bouncing and dancing, I started to roll hard. Dominic sat shirtless in a green pleather chair in the corner of the room watching me. Before long, I was rolling around on the floor in a heroin-like state while he showered. When he got out of the shower, I asked him if I looked like I'd shot up.

"Your pupils look like saucers," he said.

I've never taken heroin nor would I, but they say it's supposed to be the best high ever. So good that you should never touch it. But I can't imagine anything feeling better than ecstasy. Especially after the second hit. Unfortunately, Dominic puked up his pills in the shower and lost his high. I was rolling and he wasn't. I couldn't believe it. Keith and I never had this problem. We always rolled in perfect empathetic harmony.

Nevertheless, we pulled ourselves together and walked to the Third Street Promenade. I got a heaping scoop of peanut butter cup ice cream at Ben & Jerry's, and we even passed Jenica on the street. I hadn't seen her since grad night with Jemel. Before she was ever on sitcoms. We made eye contact but didn't acknowledge each other, oddly, even though we'd been besties in high school. After a bit, Dominic wanted to go back to our room and "relax." I think all the people were getting to him. Just like he told me they would.

We went back to the room and put on some Hooverphonic. *A New Stereophonic Sound Spectacular*. We didn't have sex. Keith and I always made love after we rolled. It was tradition. But Dominic was having some weird come-down side effects and kept twitching uncontrollably, making it difficult for me to fall asleep. Not just that, but my back ached ferociously which never happened before.

The next morning we grabbed some McDonald's and a Coffee Bean ice blended with two add shots. The extra espresso brought the ecstasy back into effect which is always nice. Ended up spending the rest of the day at Dominic's cousin Jim's house watching tv. We watched one of our Triad shows, *Beyond Chance*, which was cool. I'd never seen an episode before. We even had sex a couple times on the couch in Jim's den. Around 9:00

p.m. we went back to his apartment and crashed. It was great weekend save for the puking of the pills.

When Dave and I discussed the Dominic situation last Friday night during my closing shift at Borders, I could tell he was displeased. For the first time with Dave, I caught a whiff of jealousy. He even said he thought Dom was "cheesy looking."

I couldn't disagree.

I didn't realize what Dave was doing when he kissed me on the cheek the night Dominic and I were in the bookstore and he happened to be there. Dave explained that he was reimagining the scene at the Air concert, giving Dom a taste of his own medicine. See how he likes some random dude flirting with his girlfriend right in front of him. When I made the connection, Dave and I laughed hysterically.

Some news about Keith. Apparently, Geisinger went into the Pig last Friday night and recognized him behind the espresso bar. While Geisinger was enjoying a cup of coffee with some power lesbian friends, Keith allegedly said to him, "Hey. Do you remember me? We met the Air show."

"Oh hey," Geisinger allegedly replied. "Sure, I remember you. You were with Destiny. How's it going?"

"It's going great, man. Good to see you," Keith allegedly said. I found Geisinger's story dubious at best. First, that Keith even recognized him and second, that he would go out of his way to reintroduce himself when they barely spoke that infamous night at Air. Keith's such a phony baloney. I can clearly see all of that Mr. Cool bullshit is compensation for the fact that he's a big dick. The big dick between his legs notwithstanding.

That's why I don't want to go in there ever again. I don't want to be subjected to his fake *how you doing* routine. I would hope that he'd stay away from me completely if I did step foot in there. It's been seven weeks since that horrible night Jonathan and I were in. The only reason I haven't gone in with Dominic is that I wouldn't want to make Dom uncomfortable. And if Keith came up to us and tried to play Mr. Cool, I think I'd talk some shit.

As far as Dominic goes, I honestly can't say a bad thing about him right now. He's been a total gentleman these past couple of weeks. He's wanted to see me every night and invited me out to dinner with his mom and aunt tomorrow. Dave, whose mom happens to be a shrink, says this is the "courting period" where he lures me in and makes me fall in love with him. He believes Dominic has long-term plans for me—possibly marriage—and that if I ever wanted to get rid of him it would be difficult.

I asked Dave, "How could Dominic be so crazy about me yet not even know me?" As always, he had a response in French: "Le hommes tombent amoureux de leurs yeux. Les femmes tombent amoureuses de leurs oreilles" which translates to: "Men fall in love with their eyes. Women fall in love with their ears."

*** 

**Wednesday, April 26, 2000**

Dear Diary,

Dominic and I seem to be on the outs. The cruel way he hung up on me Monday night really pissed me off. I called his voicemail at work and told him never to speak to me again. "Let's be courteous to one another at work, but don't ever talk to me again." It infuriated me because I was attempting to have a serious conversation with him when he slammed the phone down. What I told him before he hung up was that I didn't feel we had anything in common besides sex.

But yesterday morning he brought me a box of chocolates and a long-stem read rose to work. When I got home, I threw his gifts away. I don't know why. I just don't feel like it's something to take seriously. He's not someone I can take seriously. I can't even talk to him. Everything's a prank, all fun and games, and the only time he's focused is when sex is involved. It's lonely and exasperating.

My instinct tells me he's a cheater, and I refuse to go through it. I like him as a person but can't imagine being in a serious relationship with him. He's "too unreliable" as Tom so precisely put it on the phone last night.

"If you married Dominic," he said, "you'd be over here at least once a week pissed off about something."

I laughed out loud. He's probably right!

Now Dominic's not talking to me and kind of moping around the office. He called the reception desk earlier and asked if I wanted my alarm clock back. He couldn't get the time right on it since his electricity went out. I told him to bring it into work and I'd fix it for him.

I guess we're done. He called me incessantly when he was in Chicago last week. At least two or three times a day. Was he feeling guilty about something? And what about all that great ecstasy he was allegedly doing? Don't tell me he wasn't getting happy with somebody if he was rolling like he claimed to be. Give me a break.

But he acts like *I'm* the one not to be trusted, and that drives me crazy. Ironically, I ain't doing shit wrong. I'm an innocent woman for once. Jeez, he just called and asked if I'd come back to audio. When I hesitated, he hung up on me.

What's this guy's fucking problem?

And Keith. What's up with him calling me again? I emailed him Monday: *Thanks for the Easter greeting.* That's all I said. I'm still not going to call him or ever go into the Pig. He's got to want me to call him though he hasn't said to in his messages. The one he left on Monday sounded like the ones he used to leave me back in the day. Strange. I suspect he's lonely and realized he made an enormous mistake dumping me like that. There's definitely a part of me that wants to talk to and see him, but I don't think I should. Cynthia screamed at me not to.

As far as Dominic's concerned, Cynthia said today that he and I'll be back together in a week. She said something else interesting that she's said before. When talking about whether or not I'd call Keith, she snapped, "Can't you be single for a fucking week?" It hurt my feelings.

But does she have a point?

I reminded her of how crazy she acted when Tom was staying with Jeannie while they were separated. That shut her face.

***

**Sunday, September 25, 1994**

My Eternal Destiny,

It's 11:45 p.m. I decided to write late tonight. It was nice to talk to you today. It's been almost three weeks since I left you on that sidewalk in New York City. Hard to believe. A lot's transpired in the short time since. I'm glad to hear you're in better spirits. Don't worry or be insecure about anything. We're/you're doing fine, and it's not much longer until we're back in each other's arms.

I just finished listening to the new Neil Young album. The one dedicated to Kurt Cobain. It's amazing. Reminded me of you. I'm currently listening to Jimi Hendrix's *Axis: Bold as Love*, another album that reminds me of you. Hell, everything reminds me of you! While I listened to Neil Young, I filled out all my bills and plan to distribute them to my customers today. If I get all the money I'm owed it should be close to $300. That'll be nice to put in the bank for our future. I love you. You should get the pictures tomorrow. I can't wait to hear your reaction to them. There's a beautiful one of us kissing. Your golden brown hair is blowing in the wind. I'm framing that one tomorrow.

I read chapter three of *The Power of Myth* tonight. "The First Storytellers." That man was truly amazing. I never cease to be amazed by the wisdom he possessed. Whenever I read that book, I think of you and it makes me happy. That book and his concept of *following your bliss* inspired you to become an actress, and I intend to remind you of that whenever we find ourselves navigating troubled times. Like now. I'll always be here for you, Destiny. I know you're tormented with all kinds of doubts about yourself and about life, but never doubt that. I love you more than you think.

90

Our Jimi Hendrix song just came on: "Think we better wait 'till tomorrow!" Remember? I sure do. I used to sing it all the time and you'd make fun of me. It was early in our relationship.

*Oh, Dolly Mae, how can you hang me out this way?*
*On the phone you said you wanted to run off with me today*
*Now I'm standing here like some turned down serenading fool*
*Hearing strange words stutter from the mixed-up mind of you*
*And you keep telling me that uh...*

*I think we better wait till tomorrow*
*What are you talking 'bout?*
*I think we better wait till tomorrow*
*No, can't wait that long*
*I think we better wait 'til tomorrow©*

Those were beautiful days. Actually, all of our days together have been beautiful and the greatest gift ever bestowed upon me. I wish that you believed me.

Remember when we'd hang out at College of the Desert and drive around everywhere? You had play rehearsal at 6:00 p.m. in Palm Springs those days if I recall. You'd always get an egg salad sandwich for lunch at school before switching to tuna. You'd also get one of our favorite California yogurts with Stacie before literature class. It seems like we went to Shelly's an awful lot back then. We ate a lot of breakfasts at Baker's Square and Coco's. Garden burgers, too. That was also the height of our veggie cheese melt era.

When did we stay at the Westward Ho? I'm thinking it was early December. I remember it was rainy, windy and cold as hell that day. We didn't know whether or not we were going to be able to stay there because people owed me money, and I had none. Finally got some cash that evening. That was the first time we ever got a room together. Making love in our vehicles off the side of Indian Avenue was getting uncomfortable.

I remember how relieved you were when *Not Now, Darling* was finally over. We went to the cast party in Mission Lakes Country Club, and you got the award from Herb for the most hairstyles. What did you do with that award anyway? I can't wait to eat a barbeque chicken patty melt at TGI Friday's with you again. I can't believe the one on Broadway we went to closed down. Business must've sucked or something.

Do you remember the night I skipped class and you told me all about your tempestuous relationship with Jemel? Your song just came on: "She's So Fine." I've been wanting to hear this song for a while now. I remember us sitting in my car by the baseball field at COD talking about that for hours. It was one of our first great conversations.

Another memory is the time we took our first drive out in La Quinta. It was right before you moved out of the compound for good. We drove by the Coachella Valley Cemetery, PGA West, stopped at AM/PM for some chocolate soft serve then went to my house at Vista Paseo. We discussed some crap about how we couldn't be together. I remember saying, "It's probably best we're not together because we'd have entirely too much fun" or something like that. I was right.

Oh hey...I was rummaging through my pictures the other day and found some of the ones we took in Redlands. Those are some great pictures. The black and white ones we took at Coffee Connection and on State Street. I just love the ones of you with those black sunglasses we swiped from Harris' in the mall after sucking down a Coke and iced mocha. I especially love the topless one of you in the cemetery. Your skin looks like porcelain and velvet.

That night at Shelly's just came to mind. It was close to Thanksgiving. We stopped at Vons in Palm Springs and grabbed a bottle of Martinelli's. We took a long hot shower together while we drank the chilled apple cider. We made love twice—once after the shower and once in the morning. I remember getting blood stains from my knee on Shelly's pristine white sheets. That was bad.

But my God, was that night with you wonderful. The way her down comforter enveloped our naked bodies intertwined. I had to do my paper route though. That was the only shitty part. We got to sleep in that Friday morning though, because we didn't have school. Remember we saw

*Carlito's Way* that night after a cappuccino and Coke at Harley's? I've been writing for almost an hour. Writing to you is like talking to you—the time just flies on by.

I just remembered Thanksgiving night at Vista Paseo when our fathers met. They bonded over fond memories of the Mustang Ranch. That was weird! Remember how that creeped you out? We drove to Indio afterward. All the lights were off and I was sure Phil wasn't there. You came in with me, got your stuff out of his room, and we darted down the stairs and into the kitchen before departing. That was the last time you ever set foot in that house. Now I remember, we were going to see Janos and Linda in La Quinta, so we stopped by the compound first so you could get your stuff.

I loved those times we'd eat at Baker's Square with Sheilagh and Aaron. We sure had fun with them during *The Rimers of Eldritch*. The only thing that sucked about those days was neither of us had any money. We were always broke. We had to scrounge money for Taco Bell and were always picking out of the bins at Vons. We had a blast walking and talking while we were hunting for cans though. Shit man, we collected a lot of cans. Remember the time when we were going to stop by Kathy's apartment and those people had put all the cans out with their trash, so we took them and went to Lucky instead?

Then there was Disneyland. Could there have been a more perfect day? The drive was a dream. Listening to you tell stories with Def Leppard on deck. Remember lip-synching *Hysteria* to me on that drive? I was so impressed with how well you knew the lyrics. I can't wait to see them live with you one day. I'm jealous that Phil got to but I haven't. One day.

Back to Disneyland. We get there, we pay, we start with Star Tours and then Space Mountain. Those were the two longest lines until the end of the day with Splash Mountain. We had Pirates all to ourselves. Fantasmic was impressive. Cold but edible Mexican food near Big Thunder Mountain Railroad. The Haunted Mansion was best I'd say. Actually, no. Pirates of the Caribbean is still the best since we had the boat all to ourselves. The whole day there were no lines; we did as we pleased. Took pictures—a lot of great ones I might add. Especially on that staircase in New Orleans

Square. The drive home went smoothly. We stayed at your house and made love before falling serenely asleep. It was a totally perfect day.

My hand's starting to get tired so I'm going to go now. I've been writing for an hour and a half. I just wanted to say that I love you dearly and don't want you feeling insecure. We're going to live together, get married and have a happy, fulfilling life. Don't fret. Think of me instead.

Your eternal friend and future hubby,
Matthew Ian

P.S. When you get weak and you need to test your will
When life is complete but there's something missing still
Distracting you from this must be the one you love
Must be the love whose magic touch can change your mind
Don't let another day go by without the magic touch

When you're confused and the world has got you down
When you feel confused and you just can't play the clown
Protecting you from this must be the one you love
Must be the one whose magic touch can change your mind
Don't let another day go by without the magic touch

The morning comes, there's an odor in the room
The scent of love, more than a million roses bloom
Embracing you with this must be the one you love
Must be the one whose magic touch can change your mind
Don't let another day go by without the magic touch

Shadows climbing the garden wall
Upon the green, the first leaves fall
It's the prime of life and the king and queen

Step out into the sun

Are you feeling alright?
Not feeling too bad myself
Are you feeling alright, my friend?

This time I will take the lead somehow
This time you won't have to show me how

-*Change Your Mind*: © Neil Young

***

*"People say that what we're all seeking is a meaning for life. I don't think
that's what we're really seeking. I think that what we're seeking is an
experience of being alive, so that our life experiences on a purely physical
plane will have resonances within our innermost being and reality, so that
we actually feel the rapture of being alive. That's what it's all finally
about, and that's what these clues help us to find within ourselves."* ©

## Friday, April 28, 2000

Dear Diary,

I'm never saying "never" again! Last night, Richard and I went into the
Pig and saw Keith. Since he's been calling me, I felt comfortable going in
there. Beforehand, we stopped by my apartment and threw back a quick
glass of Bailey's. Liquid courage. Richard's reaction to his very first sip of
my favorite liquor: "It's like candy!"

When we got to the Pig, Keith spotted us while we were still
outside. He came right out and greeted us. He didn't appear to be the same
guy Jonathan and I encountered not long ago. Probably because I've never

95

fucked Richard. When he came back to us before we were seated outside on the patio, he handed me a mixtape he'd made.

"I was going to mail it to you," he said, all smiles. An incredible compilation: Death in Vegas, Lou Reed, Morcheeba, The Beta Band, and even Supreme Beings of Leisure. He was very friendly. Seemed happy to see me. Almost like he'd been expecting us.

"You look good," he declared as he approached us. He looked good, too. As we ordered our drinks, Richard and I agreed that he's way cuter than Dominic. We both got mochas. Mine with whip and a shot of Bailey's. Thank God for Richard. He made me feel comfortable about going in there. He said that in order to truly get over what happened between Keith and I, I have to "confront" it. Only then, when I face it, can I release the pain and anger inside.

Honestly, I only went in there because Keith called me. Had he not called twice recently I wouldn't have set foot in the joint. Not so much as my big toe. I don't care how good their coffee is. There are decent alternatives. Thankfully, I didn't experience any overwhelming feelings of longing or wanting to get back together. Neither was there any searing pain like the time Jonathan and I were in. That was horrible. I told Richard last night that I miss talking to Keith so much.

"What I'd give to take some ecstasy and hang out with Keith again," I confessed. Richard brought up an interesting point about ecstasy and the men I attract.

"Don't you think it was telling that Dominic threw up his pills when you got that motel room in Santa Monica?"

"What do you mean?"

"I mean that by puking up the ecstasy, it proved that you and he are on entirely different levels."

"I hadn't thought about it that way, but it makes sense."

When I had dinner with Susanna from Borders a few nights back, she brought up something else important I hadn't thought of. "It sounds like

Dominic's very selfish in the relationship, only thinking about his wants and needs, and not really concerning himself with your feelings or what you might want or need," she said.

And she's right. It's all about him. That's the thing about it that frustrates me most. Feels like I keep hitting a brick wall. The fact that I can't communicate with Dominic is killing the high for me. He doesn't listen. He doesn't give a shit. He strolled through reception a little bit ago and asked how my belly was, but it's not like he really hears what I say back. I watched him closely and I could see plain-as-day he wasn't actually listening to what I said. About my achy belly or anything else. He fakes it. He's a faker. A conman. Dom the con. Full of bullshit. Completely and totally unreliable.

Oh, how I could communicate with Keith. He, who listened with body and soul. That fusing of our hearts and minds was a drug in and of itself. Ecstasy, merely a metaphor.

\*\*\*

**Wednesday, May 3, 2000**

Dear Diary,

I just got off the phone with Dominic. I've been talking to him for an hour about things. It was probably the best conversation we've ever had. I feel sad right now though. Like, unusually terrible. I wish he'd have asked me to come see him or something. Said he was going to do laundry and get some Tylenol for his headache. Maybe he's through with me. I don't know.

What I do know is that I'm severely depressed right now. I'm sure it has something to do with all the alcohol I've consumed since I got home from the bookstore—three glasses of Bailey's and counting. Delicious poison. I felt comfortable calling him because he asked me to come see him back in audio today. When I went in there he handed me a flower and said, "I want to give this to you even though you don't love me." But he didn't ask me to come over so that dreadful feeling of rejection is wrapping itself around my neck once more. I don't know if he's actually rejecting me, but I feel rejected.

Why do I always feel rejected?

I'll have to wait for my laundry to finish before I can go to sleep, even though I want to go to sleep right now. Forever. I know most of this is the alcohol talking. I'm just lonely, a feeling I do my best to avoid. I guess Dominic isn't the right guy for me either. I need someone who's patient, compassionate and mature. He's neither patient nor compassionate nor even slightly mature. So why do I give a fuck? He said he misses me but didn't try to see me. I guess he gave up too easily. Maybe he's already got someone else. Shit, now I'm crying. It's 9:27 p.m.

Cynthia drives me fucking insane. The other day she snapped at me again, "Can't you be single for a week?" It hurt my feelings the way she said it. Condescending and shrill. But does she have a point? I can't seem to be single for a day much less a week. Why? What am I so afraid of? Being in a relationship is torture for me but it really is like I'm addicted. I don't get it. I just wish she could've said it in a kinder way and we could have talked about it. It's never what you say, it's how you say it that counts. She's not very good at delivering sensitive information with tact.

I talked to her on the phone today and she aggravated me again. She aggravated me on the phone yesterday, too. I've never known such a negative person in all my life. Except for maybe Pops. I wish I could tell her that, but you can't tell her anything. She flips out. She can criticize you all day long, but if you dare utter the slightest critique of her behavior, she attacks. She even attacks when you offer positive information. Like when I told her that I was promoted to Stu's assistant at Triad. What does she say?

"Get *me* a job there!" Not "Congratulations, Destiny, you don't have to work a shitty retail job anymore" or anything nice like that. She's too fucking self-centered. It's all about her.

It's amazing how well I'm able to keep myself together day to day when I'm so fucked up inside. Sometimes the loneliness and despair are more than I can bear. I know it's the Bailey's talking right now. Although, to a great degree, this is the true me, how I feel deep down. Not so deep down? I wanted Dominic to say, "Destiny, I'm in love with you. I'm here for you. Let's work this out." But he didn't and that's why I'm so depressed.

What's wrong with me? Will I ever see the light? I just started listening to the mixtape Keith made for me. Will I get even more depressed? Is that possible?

***

**Tuesday, September 27, 1994**

To Destiny, My Love,

Talking to you today was a bundle of mixed emotions. It was nice to have a good talk with you. Just like old times before you left for school. On the other hand, it hurts me so much to hear you miserable and depressed like you are. You kept saying, "It's all clear to me now. Everything's clear." I hope that brings you some solace. All I know is that I love you, and I'm here for the long haul.

You're fast asleep I'm sure. It's almost 2:00 a.m. your time. I wish I could convince you that things are going to be fine other than via letters and phone calls. As I've said many times before, you seem to be plagued with some heavy doubts about yourself and life in general. It pains me to hear you so miserable. Such suspicions are unnecessary. I've been hoping to call you up and hear you happy, for your sake, but it hasn't happened. I was really hoping you'd learn to like New York; that you'd find some peace in those moments you were all alone and able to think about things deeply. But it hasn't gone that way. Just remember one thing when you're down: I love you, you're mine, and I am yours alone.

How was your walk around the Village? I hope it relieved some of your anxiety. I wish I could've been there to walk with you. I don't want you to feel like you made a mistake having the abortion. I know the regret is taking hold of you right now. Please don't let it. Mentally squash it the minute it arises. You made an extremely difficult decision under extremely difficult circumstances. In situations like that, no decision is a good one. It's just one

99

we're going to have to live with and learn from. I feel shitty that it happened, but there's nothing we can do now. It was always out of our hands, so don't beat yourself up by thinking you made the wrong choice.

You're going to be happy, Destiny. Just keep your chin up and your thoughts positive. I think part of why you're so insecure is because you tend to see everything in a negative light. You don't believe in yourself enough. Why is that? Why are you so doubtful of yourself when it's obvious you have everything going for you? I hope you're able to get to the bottom of this peculiar conundrum. I want to help. As long as we're together we can conquer anything. There isn't any awful thing our love can't vanquish, so hang in there. God, I hope those pictures arrive tomorrow. They'll cheer you up. Especially the one of us kissing.

I haven't forgotten what it's like to kiss you. I could never forget. Believe in yourself, I do. I'm going to go now. I'm getting tired. I'm always thinking of you, and I can't wait to hear the verdict tomorrow about dropping your classes. I hope it goes well. Please try to cheer up. Life ain't that bad. Think of me.


Your best friend in the whole wide world,
Who you can count on for anything, anytime of day,
That loves you more than life itself,
Matthew Ian

P.S.: You called me "Matthew Ian" on the phone today just like old times. It made me so happy.

***

*"Freud tells us to blame our parents for all the shortcomings of our life, and Marx tells us to blame the upper class of our society. But the only one to blame is oneself. That's the helpful thing about the Indian idea of karma. Your life is the fruit of your own doing. You have no one to blame but yourself."* ©

# Thursday, May 4, 2000

Dear Diary,

"Give me your address. I'll come over and fuck you all night long," Mickey said to me today whilst we chatted in my cubicle. I spat out some of the Pane Dolce iced cappuccino I was enjoying when the words came out of his dirty mouth.

"Sshhh," I whispered, mortified, as I wiped driblets of foam from my chin. "Do you want John Bravakis to hear you?"

"John loves me."

"Yeah, well, I'm not as confident he feels the same about me, if you know what I mean. I just got this damn promotion. I don't want to lose it before my first paycheck."

We both laughed.

Mickey's a cute new production runner fresh out of Boston. He could easily pass as the straight younger brother of Alan Cumming, pardon the pun. Jon Kelbe in motion control hooked him up with the gig. He's worked here for a couple months now and we've been enjoying some light flirtation as of late. Having somebody cute to flirt with at work is imperative.

A minute before his audacious offer, I jokingly told him that I was horny. By "jokingly," I meant that I was half-joking. By "horny," I meant that I was lonely. You can't tell 'em you're lonely. Horny, though I detest the word, sounds more innocuous. The Dominic debacle is wearing on me and I need a distraction.

Though I was "joking" in my declaration, Mickey appeared dead serious in his response. His brazenness sparked my intrigue. "*All* night long?" I leaned in and asked him.

"Til the break of dawn, baby."

"Oh yeah?" I felt my cheeks, etc. start to flush.

"Fuck yeah," he replied, grinning ear to ear like the Cheshire Cat.

After a pregnant pause to gather my delirious thoughts, I replied with a dismissive giggle, "You couldn't handle it."

At that moment, Johnny appeared behind him. He didn't look happy. From over Mickey's shoulder, Johnny glared at me and then at Mickey, slapped him rather hard on the back and said, "C'mon, man. You've got a new run to the History Channel, and it's a rush. We don't want to piss off Susan Werbe any more than she already is. Let's go."

"No, we certainly do not," I chimed in, clapping my hands in unison. "Chop, chop." Just last week, Steve Kroopnick, the nicest (and hottest) of the three Triad executives, could be heard screaming from the conference room about what a "fucking cunt" Susan Werbe is. My little ears are still mending from the shock.

After they walked away, I couldn't help but wonder if it was divine intervention or if Johnny didn't like that Mickey was talking to me and crashed our party. Perhaps both. Either way, and in spite of my curiosity, I was proud of myself for not giving Mickey my address. I'm grateful to be Stu's assistant and don't want to do anything that might taint my reputation here. This is the most money I've ever made, and I sure as hell ain't gonna jeopardize it for dick.

Proving that rejection is the greatest aphrodisiac, Mickey reappeared a few minutes later. Once inside my cubicle, he reached into his jean's pocket and pulled out a piece of paper. "If you change your mind," he said, handing it to me, "here's my pager number." The massive bulge he was now sporting didn't go unnoticed by either of us.

Face to face with growing temptation, I felt half-compelled to use it. I am horny, as well as lonely, and would enjoy getting fucked all night long. Nevertheless, after he left for the History Channel, I tossed Mickey's number in the trash. In a rare moment of lucid sobriety, I realized that the last thing I needed was to fuck another coworker at Triad Entertainment. One was one too many.

I talked to Dave for a long time on the phone today. We mostly discussed Dominic. I told him all about our conversation last night and how depressed I felt about it. He thinks Dom is going to start playing games with me now to see if he can get to me in some way.

"What do you mean *get to me*?"

"To see if he can confuse or upset you."

"You mean, on purpose?"

"Of course on purpose. It's called *gaslighting*. But all you have to do is act like you don't give a shit. Appear totally unaffected by anything he says or does. And if you do begin to feel angry or upset in any way, which you certainly will, simply acknowledge those feelings and do nothing. Become the master of your emotions. It'll drive him crazy, believe me."

Dave's strategy sounded great in theory, but could I realistically pull it off? Somehow I doubt it. If history's any indication, I'm screwed right out of the gates. A girl can dream though.

Around 5:30 p.m. Dominic called. He left a message saying that he enjoyed our conversation last night and that he wanted me in his life.

"Call me," he said before hanging up.

Of course, I don't plan to. On the phone last night, I asked him what it was about me that he liked so much and he didn't hesitate: "You're beautiful and sweet."

"Beautiful and sweet?" I snapped back. "Is that it? That's all you got?" Dominic seemed perplexed by my line of questioning and was at an unusual loss for words. When I told Dave about it, he thought it was a lame response, too.

"Remember, you're dealing with a child," he reiterated. "And that's exactly how you should treat him. Like the petulant little mama's boy he is. Whatever you do, don't get angry with him. Just stay calm and be patient, and don't react to anything he does. Treat him as though nothing ever happened between you." Which is exactly what I intend to do. I'm not going to call him. I'm going to limit my discussions of him, too. Even with David.

You'll see.

Now, what to do about my sex offer from Mickey? I'm going to have to think long and hard about this one. Pun totally intended. I wouldn't mind fucking the daylights out of that boy from Beantown. Except, as previously mentioned, it wouldn't look good. Especially since I just got promoted. Perhaps, I should upgrade to an associate producer. Maybe an editor. Joe Keeper's kind of cute.

I mean, it's not like a runner or even some douche in audio's going to get me anywhere. I don't care what 80s rock stars he knows. I'm still a talented actress who moved to Los Angeles to pursue an acting career. I shouldn't lose sight of this fact. That's why I'm here.

Did I tell you that Mickey's an actor, too? Went to Emerson College. Damn, he's cute. And packing some serious heat from the looks of it.

*** 

**Wednesday, May 8, 2000**

Dear Diary,

Dominic gave me some bullshit melodramatic letter today about how it "killed" him to see me on Friday but that he could "feel the love" between us. He said that he was sorry for not being a better communicator, but that he could "feel the love" whenever he held me or looked into my eyes. Blah, blah, blah. This, coming from the same guy who totally blew me off last weekend when I tried to see him.

Over lunch today at Panda Express, Geisinger and I concluded that Dominic's scared to reveal his true self. He thinks that Dom does everything to hide who he really is: the way he dresses, his evasive manner, immature behavior, drugs and alcohol, etc. Which likely explains why he can't/won't open up and really talk. Geisinger's adamant that Dominic and I are totally wrong for each other.

Therefore, I'm done with him. I'm not going to play his stupid little game anymore. I'm going to surround myself with people who treat me with respect and make me feel good about myself. Relationships are supposed to make you feel good, right? It seems obvious and even elementary, but I really wish someone would have told me this explicitly growing up.

Which reminds me, I saw the coolest quote on the internet at work today. It really spoke to me:

*"We end up in toxic relationships because we don't stand up for ourselves early on when red flags occur. We let them slide, because we fear losing a companion. How long do you let disrespect and neglect go? At some point you have to develop healthy barriers for how you're going to be treated. You're responsible for your experience, nobody else is."* ©

It's like, whoever wrote it, wrote it just for me.

Speaking of toxic, it's been almost a week since I talked to Cynthia. I've absolutely no desire to call her. Dad thinks I need to give her, as he likes to call it, "the biggest leavin' alone she's ever had." Every time she and I talk, I can feel my blood pressure rise. That's not normal. That's not how a friendship is supposed to feel. A friendship should be a mutually-beneficial, feel-good experience, right? Most of the time, anyway. Not this friendship.

If these people—Dominic, Cynthia, etc.—can't treat me better, they're gone. That's all there is to it. I don't need 'em. Even Richard told me to dump the bitch. Goddamnit, I deserve to be treated better by these assholes. As good as I treat all of them. I'm not going to tolerate the abuse anymore. I owe it to myself and it's long overdue.

I'm starting to realize that I might be partially to blame for my frustration and pain. After all, I'm the common denominator in all of these scenarios. I've allowed these assholes to hurt me, and I keep going back for more. What the fuck? If that ain't the definition of insanity, I don't know what is. It's time to stop. I need to stop. I don't think I'm going to call Cynthia again. Maybe I'll get lonesome and weak, and do it, but as of 11:23 p.m. on Wednesday, May 10, 2000, I don't want to.

\*\*\*

**Wednesday, September 28, 1994**

My Sweet Destiny,

I just received the letter you wrote to me on Monday. Another two-day service. Kind of strange they're getting here so fast. Are my letters arriving there that fast? You'll have to remember to tell me. It was a beautiful letter. It made me both happy and sad to read it. Whenever I read your letters, I can always hear your sweet voice over my shoulder and it comforts me. I really miss you.

When you told me about the women you see on the street and in your classes who make you feel insecure, I was really taken aback. I didn't realize you had *that* much anger and animosity inside of you. I'm sorrier than anyone's ever been for hurting you and contributing to your pain and insecurities, but I had no idea it ran that deep. I guess you weren't kidding yesterday when you spoke of this anger. I do believe that you're an angry person in general due to all the pain you experienced when you were young. It's manifested itself in many ways: anger at me, your father, Phil, Jemel, Rick, Nick, Carrie, Jamie, Ron, Lindsey. Need I say more? You have animosity toward everyone.

There's no reason for you to be engulfed with rage when you see random women on the street. They mean nothing to me. No other woman could ever do for me what you do. I'm a lucky man for being able to spend this past year with you, and we have many more to come so cheer up. We both have issues we need to understand and work out, and I want to do so by your side. Have faith in yourself and us. It hurts my feelings that you seem to have so little faith is us.

I've come to the conclusion that I do not have a sex problem. I have hostility, for lack of a better word, toward women. I don't understand it or where it comes from. That's what the gritting teeth stuff was all about when we made love. I've thought about the early days of our relationship and how borderline violent I'd be when we'd have sex. Which is another thing that

I'm ashamed of. I hope you understand. I need strength from you now as much as you need it from me.

My great fear our entire relationship has been rejection. When I said that I wouldn't look at you twice on the street, that was completely untrue. I don't know why I said it. I found you beautiful, mysterious, extremely attractive, very sexy, and alluring. All of this the very first time we met, whenever that was. At the mall or Nick's house or wherever. I know you don't like to hear this, but you'd better start listening carefully because it's true. When I said that, I meant something else. I have a real problem communicating sometimes. I've wondered lately if I might have a learning disability. My brothers do.

I don't know, because of everything that's transpired this past month I've been at an all-time low. Everything's been excruciating for me, but I'll continue forward. I'll never leave you behind. We can work through anything. Our love is too potent and true to lose each other over character flaws and self-doubt. That would be a tragedy.

You've been talking about how you're worried that you're dependent on me. I don't think so. You need me, that's all. And I need you. Who would I be now if I didn't have you back when I had to move out of the compound, and my dad was pulling all of his bullshit? I wouldn't be half the person I am now if it wasn't for you, Destiny Jones. So take some credit, dear. Credit is due.

I'm contemplating whether or not I should call you. I think I will. Even if it's to say hello or leave a message on the machine telling you "I love you." Sometimes I wonder whether or not you believe that I really do love you. Rest assured my love, I fucking do. More than anything. More than life itself. So hang in there and call or write me back. Otherwise, I'm coming to New York to take you back home. I mean it.

Your faithful friend and partner,
Matthew

***

*"What we're learning in our schools is not the wisdom of life. We're learning technologies, we're getting information. There's a curious reluctance on the part of faculties to indicate the life values of their subjects. Mythology teaches you what's behind literature and the arts, it teaches you about your own life. It's a great, exciting, life-nourishing subject. Mythology has a great deal to do with the stages of life, the initiation ceremonies as you move from childhood to adult responsibilities, from the unmarried state into the married state. All of those rituals are mythological rites. They have to do with your recognition of the new role that you're in, the process of throwing off the old one and coming out in the new, and entering into a responsible profession."* ©

## Wednesday, May 31, 2000

Dear Diary,

It's 8:46 p.m. I'm waiting for Richard to come over. I was hoping that he and I could take a walk together this evening. There's nothing better than an evening walk around the neighborhood. Northridge always looks better at night. I find city life particularly dismal. I felt the same way when I was in New York. In the gray light of day my sorrows seem magnified. But shrouded by the night, the bleak city assumes an almost magical aura as though anything were actually possible. That's one of the things I miss most about Matthew—our evening walks.

What I'd give for a time machine right now.

I'm pretty out of it from all the Bailey's I've had. Two or three glasses already. Richard's right—it's liquid candy with a twist. And since I've got a notorious sweet tooth, it's difficult to stop pouring once I've tasted that first intoxicating sip.

Speaking of sip, I had tea with Richard on my lunch break today at the Horseshoe Café. It's the perfect meeting spot being halfway between his house and Triad. He had a cup of light roast and I had some Tazo's *Wild Sweet Orange* tea with honey, hot. It was comforting, uplifting and delightful. Just like Richard. Although coffee's my drug of choice, every so often my soul craves a hot sweet tea. Usually, when I'm feeling extra-melancholy. I'm sure it's the cheerful scent of citrus that helps lift me from my L.A. doldrums.

I enjoyed Richard's company immensely. He's as smart as he is beautiful. I think that's what bothers him the most about being a model. People assume that a pretty black boy can't possibly have a brain. Nothing could be further from the truth. He's brilliant. It's just so refreshing to have a male friend that won't try to fuck me. Although, he did tell me that the first time we met at Bookstar, I gave him a hard on in the history aisle as he, Blanche and I shelved books together. Whatever. This is why I love having gay men as friends. They're never going to show me their wieners unannounced or beg to eat my pussy. It's liberating.

It was the same with Beau, my gay best friend in high school. I spent countless half-naked nights at his little apartment in Palm Desert taking Vicodin, getting back rubs, listening to Enigma and the Tom Tom Club. Not once did he attempt to show me erect parts of his body I had no interest in seeing. There's a lot of comfort in that.

I wrote and mailed a letter to Dominic today. He's been a resident of the Betty Ford Center for almost two weeks now. I went and saw him on Sunday when I was in the desert, but we didn't part of good terms. After I told him in the cafeteria that he was "unavailable," it was straight downhill from there. Then Johnny arrived mid-argument, so Dom and I couldn't finish our conversation. It was probably for the best since it wasn't going anywhere. I ended up sending Dominic a card on Monday and a "full-fledged" letter today. I reiterated that I needed more from him than I was getting. "Physically, emotionally, intellectually, etc."

It's 9:50 p.m. I just got off the phone with Richard. We're not walking but did have a wonderful conversation these past fifty or so minutes. He and Michael are hanging out at a friend's house in Chatsworth. Michael, Richard's roommate/lover, and I chatted briefly about ecstasy. He's a huge proponent. Gay men are simply the best!

\*\*\*

## Sunday, June 4, 2000

Dear Diary,

I don't know how it happened but last night and this morning, I had sex with Johnny. My former boss. The dude who hired me at Triad. No, this isn't a joke. I can't believe it either.

Friday afternoon at work he invited me to do ecstasy with him and go hiking. I thought it was strange that he asked, but you know me and E. I swear, it never crossed my mind that anything sexual could or would happen. I never got the sense he was attracted to me in the least, and I certainly wasn't attracted to him. I thought it would be a chance for us to bond on a deeper level. I had no idea how deep that bonding would go.

I arrived at his place at 4:00 p.m. sharp and we immediately swallowed our pills before departing on foot to the canyon near his Fairfax apartment. Once we got to the top of the hill, we marveled at the gorgeous sparkling panorama of the city. From above, as the sun falls, Los Angeles is beautiful. Never mind the broken souls and shattered dreams littering its streets. Up here at dusk, anything's possible.

As the drug began to take effect, we started noticing all the twinkling lights that blanketed our magnificent view. The whole scene reminded me of the glorious nights Keith and I would sit on the roof of his Silverlake apartment telling secrets until the night rolled into the day. I was simultaneously happy and sad. Lonely and content. How could such antithetical emotions concurrently exist in one body?

We sat up there for quite some time. Rolling, marveling and chatting the light away. We talked about the city and how hard it is to find someone here. He expressed "feelings of loneliness" due to his "high standards." I couldn't quite relate. Wasn't sure if it was because I had no problem finding someone or because I couldn't quite identify with the notion of "high standards" per se.

When it started getting chilly we walked back to his place. There, he thought it wise to add some Vodka to the SOBE drinks we'd acquired on our journey. We sat on his balcony sipping them, continuing to bask in our mutual ecstatic melancholy. I should've caught on to the fact that his suggestion of giving each other massages was suspect, but I didn't. I was too high. So, like a beautiful little fool, I laid on the floor and he proceeded to rub my back. After about an hour I got in his papasan chair, propped my bare feet up and he squirted oil all over them before taking them in his soft hands. Talk about ecstasy.

Did I tell you he has the same birthday as Matthew?

As good as his pleasuring of me was feeling, I suggested that we take another walk around the city. I needed air. In so doing, we both realized how his quaint neighborhood reminded us of *Back to the Future*.

When we returned an hour later, the ecstasy was beginning to wear off. Feeling ourselves start to come down, he suggested that we smoke some weed. I've never really done it before save for those couple of times with Keith, but gave it a try. From a huge bong. Three massive hits. The next thing I know, I'm sprawled out on his floor praying that I live through it.

In the middle of one such petition, Johnny lied next to me and began caressing my hair, assuring me everything would be alright. I could barely move or speak. The pot had incapacitated me. From my vulnerable place of total helplessness, I began to get aroused. My body isn't accustomed to positive touch and really comes alive in those rarefied moments.

My earliest memories of touch were either no touch at all or of being beaten by my father with pieces of wood or his leather razor strap. Pops kept two types of weapons on hand that he'd brandish anytime I said something he didn't like. I never got a warning. I got a brutal whipping at the first sign of fault. Usually when I said something that made him angry. He could explode at the drop of a hat, and I was on the receiving end of his violent rage more times than I deserved.

I have no memories whatsoever of any positive touch from my mother either. Although she didn't beat me, she never touched me either. So to be in such a defenseless position and to then be touched in such a way that

111

you're literally dying to be would render anyone aroused. I can't say that I was particularly attracted to him, but that didn't matter. The more he touched my ravenous flesh, the more attracted I became.

\*\*\*

## Thursday, September 29, 1994

Dear Destiny, My Love,

Where to start? Yesterday was a long day. We talked on the phone but you hung up when your father got on the line. I called back right after and left a message. Did you hear it? Were you in the room? Probably. Your mom said she called and left a message when your father and I ran to Vons. I hope you're not thinking the three of us are working against you. Nothing could be further from the truth.

I received your letters yesterday. In one of them you admitted that you're taking your frustrations out on me because of all the stress of being separated, pregnant, etc. You also mentioned that on the phone Tuesday night. I think you've extended that frustration to your father. Please remember that he loves you very much and supports you no matter what. There's no reason to be at odds with the two of us.

Your deep-seated anger is going to take a lot longer than 2 ½ months to work through. It will only reveal the tip of the iceberg. You're miserable. The pregnancy and abortion compounded this misery and the stress has manifested into a severe case of disillusionment. It's okay. You can come home, Destiny. It won't be a defeat. Did we expect you to go to New York pregnant? Hell no. You went to that clinic and endured a traumatic surgery. How is any of this failure? It's not. When we talked on the phone Monday you kept saying, "Things are much clearer to me now." When we talked yesterday it seemed as though that clarity had receded.

Honestly, I think you should come home. You can work at the bookstore and see a therapist. Money's not the issue and you know it. *You're* the issue. We need to pull things back together. It'll all work out fine. Just

112

be strong and hang in there. This month has been so goddamned stressful I don't know how we made it through. I can't concentrate on shit. I can't focus on reading or studying for tests. It's a gut-wrenching pain having you like this so far away. Just remember one thing: I love you very much and so do your parents.

You've been particularly hostile toward your father and myself lately. Please stop this. It's too painful for us. His feelings were hurt yesterday as were mine. I know you're in pain but this isn't right. You should be reaching out to us in a time like this not pushing us away. Your mom said that when she talked to you on Tuesday you were complaining about how men are all alike. Why are you thinking this way? Are you *that* miserable? Is someone influencing you?

If you're still talking to your roommates who have absolutely no idea about your situation and have no place to say anything, please stop and just come home. Your mom and I both commented yesterday on how there hasn't been but two or three days that you've been positive and cheerful back there. Just about every time we talk to you, you're miserable, negative and wanting to come home. Just do it. Swallow that pride. No one cares, Destiny. Take your own advice and forget what other people think. If they don't mean anything to you then why are you so worried about what they're going to think now?

We've been together almost a year. We showed them once, we'll show 'em again. You think that I'd let anyone say anything negative about you? No way. I don't care what anyone thinks or says. So why should you? I love you, Destiny. Things will work out fine. Just come home. There isn't any reason for you to stay until December 22$^{nd}$. It won't be a defeat. Staying until then is just going to drag all this out longer than need be.

I've decided not to call you for a couple of days. It's best if you call me when you're ready to talk. You're under a lot of pressure and I don't want to aggravate things further. Don't ever feel insecure as to whether or not I want to be with you. Or that I love you. Never doubt either. I want you more than anything and am willing to sacrifice anything to have you. We're going to get through this, and I can't wait to see how wonderful it is when you return and all of this is finally in the past.


Your love and best friend in the whole wide world;
Who's anxiously awaiting your return with coffee in hand;
Sending lots of love,
Matthew Ian

***


*"Love is the burning point of life, and since all life is sorrowful, so is love. The stronger the love, the more the pain."* ©


## Thursday, June 8, 2000

Dear Diary,

I'm just getting around! Last night, Mickey and I had dinner at Red on Beverly. I thoroughly enjoyed the juicy free-range chicken while Mickey savored their ahi tuna. Afterwards, we went back to his super nice apartment on Gardner and made out for a couple of hours. NEWS FLASH: I didn't fuck him! I kept the magic pussy mostly out of sight. Didn't even get undressed if you can believe it.

He wanted to have sex bad, so I compromised and let him finger me until I was running down his arm and dripping onto the hardwood floors. I'd made up my mind that we weren't going to have sex and actually stuck to my plan. He had to settle for dry-fucking me on the living room floor to Moby's *Play*.

Johnny was sitting in my cubicle today and as I looked at him, it hit me for the first time how good-looking he is. I never saw it before. He actually has a gorgeous face. Those yellow eyes—beautiful. He treats me so differently now. His golden eyes literally light up when I'm around. He invited me to go to a party at Pete Ritchie's house on Saturday night. Maybe I'll take Richard. Whenever I think back to our night together, I can't help but recall how nice it was. We definitely "made love." When he and I had lunch together at Whole Foods, I told him I was worried that by sleeping with him, it would make him think less of me.

"No way. It makes me like you more," he said.

It's the magic pussy again.

As I munched on a salad and nursed an iced cappuccino, we debated telling Dominic. Johnny said that we should definitely tell him if we decide to "see each other again." To think that for a huge chunk of my life I felt like the most unattractive, unwanted thing on this little ball of real estate spinning through space, and now they're throwing themselves at me.

When I talked to Blanche about it on Sunday night, she had me convinced I'd been used. She was certain that Johnny was getting even with Dom for something. "I bet Dominic fucked someone Johnny liked," she theorized.

I didn't want to tell her, but I didn't see it. After the way he touched and kissed me, no fucking way. Nobody's ever touched me like that. Not even Matthew or Keith. It was some serious shit. I didn't feel an ounce of revenge in that dick as it glided in and out of me with the greatest of delicacy. He'd wanted to do that for a long time. And ever since our Whole Foods lunch, my suspicions have been confirmed.

Needless to say, these be weird times.

I guess Dominic will be back from Betty Ford in a week or so. Johnny and I still haven't decided about whether or not to tell him. He seemed to think that the three of us were mature enough to handle the sticky situation. I told Johnny about that time Dominic said to me and I quote, "If you ever fuck anyone else at Triad, I'll never touch you again." I tried to convince Johnny that Dom was a jealous one, but he dismissed it. He obviously wants to tell him for some reason. He also agreed that Dom and I weren't right for each other at all. Even Mickey said last night that he thought the whole thing with Dominic and I was weird.

"But hey," Mick said, "you guys had some great sex so you got *something* out of it." I don't know how great it was, but whatever.

Wait, how would he know what kind of sex we had?

\*\*\*

**Tuesday, June 13, 2000**

Dear Diary,

I can't believe it. Keith spent the night last night. He called around 11:00 p.m. and we talked for an hour. He said he wanted to see me, so I told him to come over. Though slightly strange, it was as if no time had passed. He got here shortly after midnight and we talked, and kissed, and tried to make love but I was too sore. Ovarian cysts.

He told me he loved me more than once and explained that he felt like we were partying too hard, not really talking anymore, and this got him depressed. He admitted that he'd abandoned me in a hurtful way, and that there were times he called but got scared and didn't leave a message. He said that he was afraid to talk to me, and that he'd get angry when I'd go into the Pig after our breakup.

As we tried making love, despite the pain it was causing me, he said that he hasn't had sex with anyone else. I didn't respond. We held each other all through the night and didn't get too much sleep. As we were lying there, I told him how in love with him I am. It's undeniably true. But remember when Matthew appeared out of the blue in order to use me? I feared this was repeat of that anguish.

When I was leaving for work this morning he said he wanted to see me again, so we made tentative plans for Sunday. Richard was thrilled when I told him about it. I'm happy, too. It's just a little surreal right now. As devastated as I was when Matthew left, Keith's abandonment of me was like a gut punch. Agonizing and unjust. More karma, I suppose. Unlike with Matthew, I did nothing to deserve Keith leaving other than being completely honest about my life.

But I'll tell you this: when he was in my arms, no one else existed. Not Dominic. Not Johnny. Not Mickey. Not even Matthew. No one.

***

**Friday, September 30, 1994**

My Sweet Destiny,

I just got home from seeing your parents. Your mom's all moved in. It's a nice apartment. It's pretty small but you can't beat the price. She should be fine there. It's an old motel. *The Biltmore*. This week I'm going to be taking some pictures of it and will send them to you.

I received your card. It's a great one. Tomorrow's the first of the month. Can you believe it? Exactly one year ago we all moved into that wretched house at 46405 Willow Lane aka "The Compound." You, Phil, me, Jamie, and Ron. If we would've known then what would ensue shortly thereafter, my God. You breaking up with Phil to be with me. What a mess. But look at us now. It created something so precious, so beautiful, so timeless that it boggles my mind every time I think of it.

It was especially nice to get your card amid all that's happened recently. It's so beautiful and optimistic. When did you send it out? Prior to when I talked to you Wednesday night? You must've. I hope you still feel the way you do in the card. It gives me hope. I'm worried about you back there. We haven't talked in two days and you were real upset again on Wednesday. I'm still here and as in love as all the times previous. I think it's best for you to call me when you're ready to talk. I don't want to continue pressuring you, and I can't take any more hang ups.

How did the meeting with the therapist go? I'm so proud of you for taking this step. Your mom called today and Vashia answered the phone. She told your mom that you'd stepped out ten minutes prior. Then your mom asked her if you went to your classes today and she stuttered and faltered a bit answering. That's what your mom said. This leads me to believe that you were there when we called. Vashia said the same things to me when she covered for you last week.

Do you not want to talk to us because you're trying to objectively decide whether or not to stay in New York and don't want any influence from us? Or are you still angry at me about the past? I hope it's not the latter. If you don't want any influences confusing you, I hope you're not seriously consulting any of your friends there. I worry about that. If you are then we deserve to be heard, too.

When do you start work? Tomorrow? I hope it goes well. That should bring a little order and stability. I hope you like it at Barnes & Noble there as much as you did here. At least that one has a café unlike Palm Desert. You must be thrilled! Please remember that my time and attention are always available to you. I love you more than life itself. We will see a million more anniversaries, so hold on and keep plugging away. I know you love me. There's no doubt in my mind. Everything else aside, you should know without a doubt that I love you madly, truly, endlessly.

You don't have to call but please write to one of us three and tell us what's happening. We all love and care for you too much to be in the dark like this. Every time I come home, I ask if anyone's called for me or check the machine for a blinking red light. Whenever the phone rings, I jump up hoping to hear your voice. I'm always with you, Destiny. Remember that. I can feel you with me always. You are alive inside me, and I'll never lose the feeling of love and devotion to you.

By the way, I still haven't forgotten what it's like to kiss you. Try to remember what it's like kissing me. It'll come back. Hang in there, darling. Everything will work out fine. I'm so very proud of you.


Your truest friend,
Matthew Ian


P.S. Please remember to tell me how long it's taking my letters to reach you. I'm dying to know. Your card and past three letters have only taken two days each. I love you. And thanks again for the beautiful card. It made me happier than I could ever describe with words. It's so beautiful. Please write back as soon as you get this letter.

\*\*\*

*"The way to find out about your happiness is to keep your mind on those moments when you feel most happy, when you really are happy—not excited, not just thrilled, but deeply happy. This requires a little bit of self-analysis. What is it that makes you happy? Stay with it, no matter what people tell you. This is what I call 'following your bliss.'"* ©

## Sunday, July 2, 2000

Dear Diary,

I had a very eventful week. First, I told Keith that I didn't want to continue seeing him. I lamented over it Monday at work. The magic wasn't there anymore and his insecurity seems at an all-time high. He freaked out because Mickey had called me, and because I had expressed some fondness for him. That's the other thing. All I could think about the entire weekend was Mick. He called on Saturday while I was at Savon and Keith was still sleeping. "Hey lover, I'm thinking about you." Then again on Sunday when Keith and I got back from Santa Barbara.

On Monday night after I told Keith that I didn't feel the same way anymore, and that there were things I wanted that he couldn't give me, Mickey came over and we finally had sex. It was great. Big dick. Loved it. Keith who? I told Mick that I couldn't take it anymore and had to have him. We did it again Wednesday and Thursday nights. Each night it got better, and in the middle of the night on Wednesday he told me that he loved me whilst pretending to be asleep.

"I love you, too." I whispered gently in his ear. In the milky coming of the day, however, it was never mentioned.

Friday after work he told me to call him, and I finally did this afternoon. When he called me back, it was kind of weird. He told me that he was at some mansion last night doing ecstasy. Where have I heard this shit before? It felt weird. It depressed me. Was it intended to? Surely not. He said he'd call me tonight but it's now 11:16 p.m. and I haven't heard a word. Oh well.

My phone rang late last night...twice...but no one left a message. I see how it's going to be. You can bet I ain't going to call him.

***

**Saturday, July 8, 2000**

Dear Diary,

I just got off the phone with Blanche. We talked for over two hours. We were supposed to go out for drinks tonight but she didn't feel up to it, so we talked on the phone instead. Richard backed out today, too. It was probably a money issue. He's been throwing me a weird vibe lately. Not sure what's up with that. He hasn't called since Tuesday and I've asked him twice to get together but he declined both times. I think I'm going to let him call me next time.

Okay, Mickey just called. He's going to come over later and we're going out for coffee. Cool. I was worried I'd have to spend the night in and alone; that fate more dreaded than death, more terrifying than impending death. Hopefully one day I can transcend it.

Until then…

I told Blanche all about fucking him and how good it was. She says she doesn't blame me for doing it. "Get it while you can," were her exact words. She just hopes he can "be cool" about it and not say anything to anyone at work. Especially since Johnny's all over me now. He asked me to call him this weekend. I wish I was interested, but I'm just not. He treats me far too well for me to have a lick of interest.

Blanche thought it was hilarious when I told her that Johnny thought he'd "seduced" me. She didn't think he'd seduced me at all. She said that I was merely "under the influence" and needed "a little tenderness." Both true.

Mickey and I had more mind-blowing sex this week. I'll be lucky if I don't get kicked out of my apartment for all the noise we've been making. He's louder than me. I've already had anonymous notes stuck to my door asking me to "keep it down." How embarrassing. I told Blanche that I couldn't take the pressure anymore and had to fuck him. She admitted that after he said, "I'll come over and fuck you all night long," anyone in their right mind would've been intrigued.

"The Gemini girl will always want to know and will always fuck around," she asserted. And that if I was still with Keith and things were cool, I probably still would've fucked Mick out of pure curiosity. She said it's difficult, if not impossible, to resist good sex, and that I should definitely enjoy it to its fullest while I can.

For once, Blanche was wrong. I didn't tell her that but she was. She doesn't know that I would never "fuck around" on anyone I was serious with again. And I haven't.

In the middle of the night on Thursday Mickey whispered, "I'm so crazy about you," as he feigned being asleep. I didn't respond this time. I do enjoy having sex with him. Though I still need to masturbate to reach orgasm, having a dick in there that fills you up in the way his does...the way Matthew's did...Keith's...makes the process of coming a lot easier. It actually hurts sometimes when he's on top of me, I love it!

I doubt I could ever get bored with our sex. I just hope we can keep it real and not get fucked up along the way. I don't want to get all attached and get my hopes up. I don't even know the guy. He could be a sociopath for all I know.

***

**Wednesday, October 5, 1994**

My Love,

What a terrible day. I don't know what more to say. I said all that I possibly could've. I'm still here if you want to work it out. You have every right to feel the way you do, so I'm not going to say much more than that. You said a couple of times on the phone, "Love isn't enough." If *love* isn't enough, then what is? Then *what* is?

You've changed a bit this month. This is what I was afraid of. You've changed enough to know that I'm not worth it, I guess. For eleven months I've had a wonderful companion who's done her best to live with my painful idiosyncrasies, and I'm grateful. I hope to God that somehow I'll get another eleven and another eleven after that. But if I don't, I'll understand. You must've already taken my pictures down. I haven't taken yours down and never will.

I went to the mall the other day. It seemed so empty without you. I couldn't even walk by Gloria Jean's Coffee Bean. I'll sit in those chairs again one fine day but only with you. I drifted into Walden Books and found *A Child is Born*. I looked at the two pages on the six-week-old baby. They said it's about 15mm (½") and that its spinal column, hands and feet begin to form at that stage. The pictures were eerie. It made me sad to see images of the happy, expectant couples. To think of those pictures as our child was kind of strange. Never again.

I hope to God this isn't the end. You were pretty mad when you hung up. I'm hurt that you had to keep talking to Vashia about our business and all, but I understand. I always do. The reason it seemed like nothing ever meant anything to me is because I always forgave you for it. I hope you can forgive me for hurting you with my thoughtless words sometime soon. You said that you "have no respect" for me. That's not true. You were in a lot of pain when we talked. So was I. I forgave you for all the hurtful things that you've said to me. That really hurt though. You do deserve better than all this, and I can be better.

It's hard for me to live with everything I've done that hurt you. I take responsibility for it. It'll just be ironic if we break up now. When I'm ready to do something about all my problems and insecurities. We've been talking about them for months, but it was never a healthy or productive conversation like it was tonight. Both of us would always get emotional because of how painful it all is.

I do want to live with and marry you. You feel that I don't because of the things I've said and how it's affected you. It's okay for you to feel the way you do, but it's just not true—that I don't really love you, don't want to marry or live with you, and don't find you attractive or beautiful. You've said all of this is irreversible. Well, if what you said to me this evening turns out to be true, I guess you were right.

I'm confused and in a lot of pain. I'm hurting because of how I've hurt you and in turn, how it's made you feel. I do feel inadequate. I feel like I'm not worthy of you like this and goddammit, I'm not. I was just hoping you could find the strength to help see me through it. I'm not asking for you to talk with me until the wee hours of the morning about all of this. To know the woman I love, who loves me for me, is supporting me would be the greatest gift. It has been for eleven months, and I'm hoping that it'll continue. I just wanted to be different than everyone else. I haven't always been. But goddamn it, I could be. Shit, I hope you've read this letter thus far.

I don't know what more to say than I love you, Destiny. I love you more than anything in the world and will give anything in the world for you. I am so, so sorry for hurting you like I have. I never meant to. You deserve better and what hurts the most is that I've known all along that I'm different. I just needed a loving, insightful, honest, and beautiful person like you to show me the way. I hope you'll continue to teach me what life is really about.

I love you, Destiny.
Matthew

***

*"The idea of the Goddess is related to the fact that you're born from your mother, and your father may be unknown to you, or the father may have died. Frequently, in the epics, when the hero is born, his father has died, or his father is in some other place, and then the hero has to go in quest of his father. Now, the finding of the father has to do with finding your own character and destiny. There's a notion that the character is inherited from the father, and the body and very often the mind from the mother. But it's your character that is the mystery, and your character is your destiny. So, it is the discovery of your destiny that is symbolized by the father*

*quest. In Star Wars, Luke Skywalker says to his companions, 'I wish I had known my father.' There's something powerful in the image of the father quest." ©*

## Friday, July 14, 2000

Dear Diary,

I didn't go to the bookstore tonight. Just wasn't up to it. Had a dreadful headache and knew it would've been torturous trying to get through the night there feeling this way. Hardly talked to Mickey at work today. Don't think I said more than ten words to him. Right when he walked in I handed him his forty dollars and said, "They ran out of tickets. Sorry." Hunter was standing there, and I didn't want him to know I was scoring drugs for Mickey. He definitely had a surprised/disappointed look on his face when I told him our little ecstasy escapade wasn't happening.

A short while later when no one was around, Mickey snuck back into my cubicle and asked me if I was bummed that my supplier ran out. I told him that I was, but that I knew someone else who could likely hook me up with a couple hits: my friend Cristina from the theater company. Nevertheless, Mickey and I didn't talk the rest of the day. When he was leaving he said, "Have a good night," and that was it. I don't want to do drugs with somebody who's not really into it. And that's definitely the vibe I got from him yesterday.

Sam and I talked tonight. I told her that I wanted to go on a weekend bender with her soon. She can bring coke and possibly acid, and I can try to get the ecstasy. I told her about Giant in Hollywood and how it's like a rave. She was intensely excited by the idea of going. If I weren't doing drugs with a lover, I'd definitely want to do them with Sam. She'd be up for anything. I need to have some fun. Let loose. This nice girl, nine-to-five shit is a killer. I've been working, working, working for so long now. It's taking a toll on me. The last real fun I had was at Air with Keith. I consider that night the last hurrah.

God, I miss doing drugs. I really wanted to get high with Mickey. I'm bummed that he acted so weird about it yesterday. Then again, he did hand me cash to get him some. I wonder if he just wanted me to get it for him to do without me. Surely not. Surely, he would have wanted to do them with me. Let's hope Cristina can come through with those two hits. I'll just take them by myself if I have to. I'll go down to the beach, listen to the Doors and roll solo. I almost forgot. When I suggested getting a room at the beach with him and doing ecstasy there, Mickey replied, "Isn't that what you did with Dominic?"

"Yeah, so what?"

I felt a little defensive. Maybe that's what bothered him, I don't know. Hunter told me today that he thought Mickey might be bothered because every time he was going to come talk to me at reception, Dominic was there. He implied that Mickey was jealous. I don't know about that. Maybe. I guess I just don't get a good sense of what Mickey really thinks or wants. Except of course, SEX. I'm certain he wants that. Now whether or not he truly likes me, I don't know. And by "likes me," I mean as more than just a m.o.m.: multiple orgasm maker.

He is fun to fuck; I have to admit. I came my brains out two or three times Wednesday night. That big dick makes it impossible not to. But it would be cool to just hang out with him, too. Like what Stephen and I had minus the alcoholism, insanity, and banging of my best friends. Hanging out and fucking: the perfect relationship.

You know what it is? Once you have sex, you feel like you can't be honest with that person anymore. Like, there's something to hide now. Like, the other person's going to take whatever you say the wrong way and assume that you want more from them than just sex. I just want my "relationship" with Mickey to be the same as it was before except that now we orgasm simultaneously.

\*\*\*

**Thursday, July 16, 2000**
Dear Diary,

I had quite the interesting night last night. First, I scored two hits of ecstasy from Trevor at Borders. Super high-quality, totally pure MDMA capsules. Popped 'em in Santa Monica after work then ambled along the boardwalk listening to The Beta Band. Wild-eyed songcraft like *Dry the Rain, Needles in My Eyes, Dr. Baker,* and *She's the One* serenaded my solitary stroll as the drug slowly started to kick in, melting my eternal sadness.

After the boardwalk, I made my way to the Third Street Promenade and wandered through some of my favorite stores. Urban Outfitters, Anthropologie, Barnes & Noble along with a few others that strangely escape me now. Curiously, I caught Kurt Russell's eye when I passed him on my way into Urban Outfitters. A split second after seeing Wyatt Earp emerge from my favorite retailer, I flashed back to the time Matthew, Pops and I saw *Tombstone* together at the Palm Desert Town Center. Shortly before I departed for NYU. My God, Val Kilmer as Doc Holiday. Such a great memory.

Was it all just a dream?

When I started to feel myself come down from the drug—that dreadful descent—I immediately acquired an ice blended mocha from The Coffee Bean, found my way back to the white Stanza and drove home to Northridge. The journey was uneventful until my right arm began to tingle intensely before going completely numb somewhere along the 405 North. It was then that I decided get off the freeway and drive to Vons for some cranberry juice.

When I got out of the car in the parking lot, I saw stars and thought I was gonna drop. Something wasn't right. Terrified, I drove directly home sans cranberry juice. Once there, I took a warm bath then laid in bed for a while. That's when the crazy thoughts began, and I started to panic...

*Am I going to die? Oh my God, am I going to die all alone in this cold little studio apartment? Who will bury me? Wait—no. I don't want to be buried. Don't you fucking bury me! Please don't leave me in a hole all alone. Please don't bury me. Worse—will anyone ever love me again? Will I be alone forever? What if everyone I love just vanished one day leaving me an orphan in a cold, cruel world?*

In the midst of my existential aneurysm, I considered calling Keith but somehow fought the gripping urge. Just as I was about to snap, to careen off the psychic precipice, the phone rang.

It was Mickey.

Motherfucker saved my life with that call. An hour later he was here. *I won't be dying alone tonight* I recall thinking. Still, I needed air. I felt claustrophobic. We spent the rest of the night driving around, listening to music, roaming random rooftops in Hollywood. The guy's fresh out of Boston yet he knows how to access several rooftops in greater Hollywood. Atop one of them, I spontaneously performed Stephen Falk's *The Coldest War* monologue for him. "Moscow, Moscow, here I come!" He told me that I was the best actress he'd ever seen.

"Ever?" I was skeptical.

"Ever."

"With a single performance?"

"Fuck yeah, baby. You're *that* good."

Somehow I believed him. After the roof-hopping, we went back to his apartment on Gardner, listened to more music then watched some video that was like being on an acid trip. Around 3:00 a.m. we drove back to my apartment and fucked like crazy until dawn. Oh my God, that dick. That huge fucking cock. If there's one thing I'll never tire of it's a huge cock buried inside me. This guy's got one for days, as thick as it is long. Knows how to use it, too. As he squeezed that thing inside of me, barely able to fit it in, the pressure seemed to bring the drug back to life.

"Your pussy's so tight."

"That's what happens when you don't have babies."

"It feels so good."

"Not as good as that big dick feels," I groaned. Never in my life have I simultaneously orgasmed with a lover like this. Mickey's a screamer, too. I've never fucked a screamer before. I'm usually the one screaming. And once again, in the middle of it all, he told me that he was "crazy" about me. He also said that he wanted to fuck me for the rest of his life. I kid you not. If it's true that women fall in love with their ears, then I was in a slow-motion freefall. As we laid intertwined and soaking wet, I started to feel something for him.

During lunch today we walked to Whole Foods directly behind Triad. I bought an Arizona Ice Tea and then we went back to my car and sucked face for the remainder of my break. He wanted to fuck right there in the parking structure, but I couldn't do it. What if John or Stu or Steve Kroopnick were to see my car all steamed up? I have *some* boundaries.

Plus, as we were leaving for lunch, I think Johnny was leaving too and may have figured out what we were doing. Maybe now he'll get the picture. By the way, Keith left a nice message on my machine tonight. He said he's trying to be my friend. Oh, and Cristina scored three more hits of ecstasy. I asked her to marry me.

\*\*\*

**Thursday, October 6, 1994**

To My Love, Destiny,

PLEASE READ THIS LETTER, THERE'S NO ANGER. These are rough days. I'm in a lot of pain right now, probably the worst I've experienced thus far. I can't sleep and my mind's incapacitated. I scheduled an appointment for next Tuesday with the woman I saw for therapy when I first moved to the desert. Remember the lady my dad and Susan made me see because they were alarmed that I had contact with females?

I'm sitting here listening to my father tell someone involved with Luke that we can't go to court on his behalf because my dad's leaving for Michigan on Tuesday. He's prioritizing Susan over his own son. I can't fucking believe this. Between my problems and the shit I put up with every day at this house, I'm going insane. My parents are continuing to bicker over whose fault it is that Mark and Luke are so fucked up.

I think my dad's behaving this way because he has no companionship. Even though Susan's a cunt, she was at least here last January. Now she's in Michigan and he's all alone. I feel sorry for him. For once, I understand how you feel about your mom. I have a lot of pain and anger because of this man—my father—but when I look at him, I can't help but feel pity. At the same time, his loneliness is the fruit of his own doing. So, what the hell can we do? Just try to be good; a good and loving son/daughter/person. The main thing we should learn from our mother and father is who *not* to be. We should give them the love and attention they didn't give to us…to a certain point.

As far as we're concerned, I'm praying that you don't really feel the way you did last night. I'm still committed to this relationship, and I know we can see this through. I'm getting help, and I know that deep down you want to work this out. We don't have to talk on the phone much. We can communicate through letters. It'll be hard, but we can do it. Shit, look at what we've been through already. All I ask is that you send a letter in response to this one. By the time you receive this, and I receive your response, everything should be well thought out on your part. If you no longer want to continue a life with me at that point, I'll stop writing and calling.

I feel like we've been jipped in a way. We've had so much pain and anguish in our eleven months together between our issues and all the problems outside the relationship. What I would give to sip cappuccinos and Cokes with you in total peace. Life's been rough on the both of us this past year. But we can make it through this and everything else if we both just believe in one another. You said yesterday that this relationship "has never been healthy." In some respects that's true, but I don't totally believe it. We've had some awful moments, but the moments that were most special showed me that we have more in us than sorrow.

It's been one month exactly since I left you on that NYC sidewalk all alone. Four excruciatingly painful weeks, but I'll continue my deepest commitment to us if you allow me to. Please write back as soon as possible. Whenever I read one of your letters, I forget everything that's happening around me. It's like a little time capsule of love.


Your truest friend,
Matthew Ian

***


*"I had an illuminating experience from a woman who had been in severe physical pain for years from an affliction that had stricken her in her youth. She had been raised a believing Christian and so thought that this had been God's punishment of her for something she had done or not done at that time. She was in spiritual as well as physical pain. I told her that if she wanted release, she should affirm and not deny her suffering was her life, and that through it she had become the noble creature that she now was. And while saying all this, I was thinking, 'Who am I to talk like this to a person in real pain, when I've never had anything more than a toothache?' But in this conversation, in affirming her suffering as the shaper and teacher of her life, she experienced a conversion—right there. I have kept in touch with her since—that was years and years ago—and she is indeed a transformed woman." ©*

**Monday, October 24, 2016**

Dear Diary,

Long time no write. How have you been, old friend? I can't believe it's been fifteen years since I cracked you open, peered inside and bared my soul. I forgot how many of my secrets you possess. Innermost thoughts and feelings. Emotional minutiae. The real me. I've spent the morning blowing thick layers of dust from your ancient outer edges. As I pressed your musty pages against my nose and took a deep breath in, I was transported back in time and space. It's funny how scent can do that.

It was the summer of 2000 when I wrote my last word here. It feels like a past life. It was. Mom had been dead for a year-and-a-half. Matthew, gone a year more than her, was already in another serious relationship, and I hadn't healed from any of it. You can't heal from a death you refuse to accept happened. I was deep in the denial phase of the immeasurable loss that engulfed me. I was only 27. Still young though hardly innocent.

I'd just begun my tempestuous 2 ½ year relationship with Mickey when I revealed my last secret here. Oblivious to the nightmare that awaited me. Mickey's real name was Michael though he refused to be associated with it for reasons we need not discuss. Mickey, Michael, Mr. *"Give me your address. I'll come over and fuck you all night long."* Ironically, he wasn't lying with that audacious assertion. But such truths, I would discover, were few and far between. Dude turned out to be the most pathological of all the liars I've encountered. A borderline sociopath. On par with Kay—the grand dame of deceivers. He liked to cheat, too. And abuse.

Ain't karma grand?

But the sex. Crazy folks can fuck 'tis true. I'm saying this with certainty as a crazy person myself. Once, when we started dabbling in cocaine per his suggestion, Mickey fucked me for sixteen hours straight in my studio apartment on Orange Street at Fairfax. The one he helped move me into when I left Northridge. I got too many complaints about our raucous love making and had to move. The new place was spitting distance from

LACMA and the La Brea Tar Pits. I loved that spot. "Beverly Hills adjacent."

We began our marathon fuck session that morning at 10:00 a.m. and it wasn't until around four o'clock the following morning that Mick would finally come. Visions of Tera Patrick's massive tits bouncing in the wind helped spur him across the finish line. We must've watched that porno twenty times on a loop. When he finally came, he blasted his wad with such force onto my weary nose that my head literally snapped back, slamming into the writing desk my father gave me for my 12th birthday.

Little did I know back then but Mick would be the last "relationship" I'd ever have. Sure, I had some fine fuck boys in the years that followed— Jeff (the oversexed anti-Christ I met online), Lopez (the well-endowed skater I met in rehab), and Tim (the sexy but married blue collar hunk I met through Mike). But never again would I have a "relationship" in the "traditional" sense.

I'd been "cured" of relationships as it were.

I should fill you in on where I'm at these days though it's hardly newsworthy. I moved back to the desert in May of 2003 after narrowly escaping the slings and arrows of life in L.A. I arrived there wide-eyed and optimistic with Matthew in late '95 and left disillusioned, broken-hearted and hooked on coke eight years later. My beloved, in Orange County with his new wife by now. I'd spend the next eleven years in this house at war with my father, rehashing everything he did and didn't do that rendered me incapable of having a healthy relationship.

I'm not the actress I'd hoped to be. I'm a barista. I've been working at Koffee in downtown Palm Springs for 2 ½ years. Koffee is the most popular café in Palm Springs. I became a customer when they opened in 2002 while I was still with Mick. In keeping with my commitment to only get jobs where I like what's done there, I applied and Troy hired me. It's the toughest job I've ever had. Not only is it hard physical and mental labor, but having to deal with the public on the scale I do there can be harrowing for an introvert like myself.

Tragically, I haven't seen nor spoken to Matthew since 1999. Last fucking century! Although, I have had countless dreams about him over the years. In most of them, we're meeting in secret to make vivid love. In all of the dreams, he's married to Julie while shamelessly having an affair with me. In reality, he's a college history professor and lives in L.A. with his family. I've resigned myself to the bitter fact that I'll likely never see him again. I think about writing him an amends letter on occasion. I want him to know how our breakup changed me, and that the hardest thing a person can ever do is mourn the death of someone who's still alive.

Maybe I'll get around to writing it one day.

Pops is ninety fucking one years old. Ornery old bastard's *still* alive! He's been in assisted living since late 2014. He started losing his marbles and falling all the time, so I had no other choice. The stress of caring for him while working at Koffee was overwhelming. I never imagined he'd live this long. I remember being a 7th grader at Precious Blood Catholic Elementary when he collapsed on a treadmill at his doctor's office. I remember being a freshman at Palm Desert High School convinced he'd drop dead any day from a heart attack. Instead, he stuck around to see my 40th birthday and beyond.

I'm grateful we've been able to repair our relationship since he moved out. Living under the same roof for eleven years was codependent, sick, dangerous. It's a miracle we didn't kill each other. Blanche used to say, "You've returned to the scene of the crime, Destiny." There were times, many times, that I fantasized about murdering him. And not with the long barrel Taurus .22 he kept under his pillow. No, I took great pleasure that bordered on the erotic imagining strangling him with a phone cord. I wanted to look straight into his blue eyes as I squeezed the ice, I mean, *life*, right out of them. But like I said, things are better. Now that he's not in this house anymore I'm at peace. I can relax; let that shit go. You have to let your shitty past go otherwise it kills you on the installment plan. It kills you and repels others. I just want this relationship with him to end with grace. I don't want my father to die and my heart be tormented with regret like it is with Matthew.

We had some coffee and pastries this afternoon at the little 1950s diner inside Windsor Court where he lives. Like me, Pops enjoys a strong cup of coffee. No cream. No sugar. No bullshit. Black as night. The diner's real nostalgic. It's lined with red vinyl booths and there's a shiny chrome jukebox near the entry. The walls are plastered with chrome framed pictures of 1950s icons: Marilyn Monroe, James Dean, Lucille Ball, and Elvis.

Sitting at one of the high top tables in the center of the diner, I decided that we needed some tunes, so I fished some spare change out of my purse, slid off my chair and walked over to the jukebox. I perused the selection, slipped my coins inside her and selected *"Don't Be Cruel"* by Elvis Presley.

"Don't you just love Elvis?" I asked Pops, gathering some coffee and pastries for us from the counter. Today's goodie was a cinnamon roll—a delightful pairing to the coffee. Not too big. Not too small. Just right.

"I always liked Chuck Berry better."

"Did you know that Mom saw Elvis live back in the day? She said the whole experience really pissed her off because she wanted to hear him sing but couldn't because of all the hysterical screaming girls."

Pops smiled and took a shaky sip of his coffee.

Determined to squeeze as much information out of him while I still had time, I took a hearty swig from my Styrofoam cup then initiated a rather somber conversation. "How'd your dad die exactly?"

"A ton of snow fell on him. It just slipped off as he and another guy were walking underneath it."

"While they were working in the mine?"

"Yeah. We didn't know the other kid. He was from North Dakota. My mother wrote to his mother but we never heard from her."

"Wrote her what?"

"To tell her we knew how she felt."

"That's the worst—a sudden death. Do you remember your last conversation with him?"

"Mmm hmm," he replied, nodding. "He'd come down from Bishop for the weekend. He had to fill his car up with gas to go back, and I rode with him up to the station. He got the car filled and we rode back, visiting like we always did."

"Do you remember what you talked about?"

"We just talked, hon."

"How long after that did he die?"

"Next day or two."

"Who broke the news to you?"

"The union," he said, taking a bite of his cinnamon roll.

"Not a family member?"

"No. They told the union to tell the family."

"Who actually said to you—*your father's dead*?"

"Jim McGraw."

"Who?"

"A business agent."

"What exactly did he say?"

"He said, 'Jim, I want you to take this like a man now. Your dad got killed today in Bishop.'"

"*Take this like a man*? What does that mean?"

"Don't get all excited."

"How did you take it though?"

"I, I...I took it without saying a word, hon."

"But how did you feel inside?"

"Christ, I loved my dad dearly. Still do."

This question appeared to upset him.

"You threw those pictures of him away?"

I had no idea what he was talking about.

"Never. Hell no."

There he goes again. Blaming me for something I didn't do. That's one thing about Pops that's burned me since I was a kid. He never believed me when I'd tell him shit. True shit. Didn't matter what it was. He'd call me a liar. I never understood it, and it tore me up inside. Or, worse—he'd blame me for shit I had nothing to do with. Whether it was breaking that ceramic Indian head or reporting that he'd molested me. I had nothing to do with either yet he blamed me for both.

Pops never molested me. His abuse was physical, emotional, mental. An evil neighbor girl made false accusations when we were in the 6th grade. But Pops was certain I'd done it to "get attention." They made him get a polygraph, everything. I remember feeling so hurt, so betrayed that my own father believed I could do something like that. This is what you call "guilt by association." Since I was Kay's daughter, and she was notorious, I had to be guilty. I never even told anybody about the beatings he'd give me much less something that wasn't true. Being accused and polygraphed was probably just his karma for that.

I think the poor girl responsible for the report may have been projecting her tragic life onto me at the time. That's what my intuition always told me. I try not to think about all that stuff these days and instead, look more on the bright side, enjoying the limited time we have left. I'll miss him when he's gone. He's the only one that never left.

"The pictures of me and him working in the mine. You sure?"

"I would *never* throw something like that away, Pops."

"Good."

"You really underestimate me sometimes, and it hurts."

I'd been waiting a lifetime to tell him that.

"How about some more Elvis?" I said. Fishing more spare change out of the bottom of my purse, I slid back off my chair toward the jukebox. I slipped the coins inside her and selected *Suspicious Minds*.

"I don't mean to," said Pops. I could hear a hint of sadness trail his words. "So, you got a day of teaching in?"

Pops is a master of the pivot.

"Substitute teaching. It was rough."

"I hope you don't quit. I hope you don't quit teaching 'em. You'd be so good at it." Suddenly I realized that my father was projecting again. *He* was the one who quit teaching *me* though he'll never connect the dots. He gave me explicit advice once upon a time about how to ensure that people like me. Advice that I took to heart and applied to life. But the guidance ended there. I could have used a little more. There was no interpersonal advice—what to tolerate and what not to in relationships of all kinds. And what about the vital importance of liking myself? I don't recall that conversation.

Perhaps he knew nothing about it.

"Here's what they wrote on the board for me." I handed Pops my cellphone with all the pictures I took on that harrowing day subbing at Condor Elementary. A day that left me so frazzled, I knew I'd never make it as an elementary teacher.

"I'll miss you forever and ever," he recited, squinting to see.

"All these little kids spontaneously started writing the sweetest things on the board for me toward the end of the day. I think they saw how rattled I was and wanted to show their appreciation. It was quite remarkable."

"Where at?"

"A 4th grade class out at the 29 Palms marine base."

"Don't quit."

"Last week. Holy shit, it was rough."

"Don't quit. I think it'll be really good for you."

"I can't quit, Pops. If I quit now, I'll be serving coffee the rest of my life. I dream of the halcyon days of yester when I was the one being served the coffee every morning, noon and night. Not the other way around."

"Good, hon. That's good."

"Have a little faith in me, goddamn it."

I'd been waiting a lifetime to tell him that, too.

"I know I've asked you this before, Pops, but when *you* die, if you can, promise you'll let me know you're there. Give me a sign. Something I can't miss. Mom did, remember? You know I like playing cards. Send me lots of cards."

"If I can."

"I have faith that you can."

Pops smiled and took another shaky sip from his Styrofoam cup.

"I've got to go," I told him. "I love you."

"I love you, too."

"Call me tomorrow."

"I will." With that, his blue-gray eyes assumed a peculiar sadness. It was peculiar because even the most subtle displays of emotion were rarefied with Pops.

*** 

**Thursday, December 8, 2016**

Dear Diary,

I'm working in Rancho Mirage now. I asked Troy for a transfer and he agreed. I couldn't bear working next to the Ace Hotel any longer. It was a constant, crushing reminder of the passionate night Matthew and I spent there when it was the Westward Ho back in '93. King's Highway was a Denny's. The man I loved, loved me.

Today was my day off so I took Pops some tobacco. He's been hounding me for days to bring him a couple cans. Drives me nuts. All those times he belittled Kay for being a "pill head" and it turns out he's the fiend. I should've known it was all projection. I'm no shrink, but I've concluded that my father possesses many narcissistic traits. Save for the braggadocios part. This gradual revelation helped explain many of the confounding things he's said, done and ignored that hurt me so. Kay was correct all along: "You're alright, kid. It's the world that's all wrong." The world, in my case, is my father James.

When I took him his fix, Pops and I had some coffee and pastries at the little 1950s diner inside Windsor Court like we usually do. Ever mindful that the clock is ticking, I presented him with another round of hard-hitting questions. Once, during a car ride in middle school, he told me point blank: "You ask too many goddamn questions." It felt like a gut punch that reverberates to this day. Nevertheless, I needed answers and the questions weren't going to ask themselves. There's so little I know about my enigmatic father.

Fishing some change out of my purse, I got up from our corner booth and walked over to the jukebox. I perused the selection, slipped the coins inside her and selected Bill Haley & His Comets' *Rock Around the Clock*, straight off the soundtrack from *American Graffiti*. Pops seemed pleased with this choice. I could tell by the way he started tapping his foot as the music began. The old man's not a foot-tapper so this was my first clue.

"What's the most important thing you've learned in life?" I asked him, taking a sip of my coffee. Though my question was profound his response was immediate, almost as if he knew I was about to ask it.

"I learned that I was allergic to alcohol from A.A.," he replied. "I didn't know that if I took one drink, I couldn't stop."

I was surprised that this was Pops' most important life lesson and waited for him to ask me the same question. He never did. The narcissist isn't interested in you. It's the strangest thing. They don't even act like they are. It's all about them. They're constitutionally incapable of giving a fuck. I often wonder if Matthew ever figured out that his dad was a narcissist, too.

Which explained why he practically ignored his three sons. Matt and I shared that sickness though we were oblivious to it at the time.

"*That's* the most important thing you've learned in your long, long life, Pops?"

"Damn straight."

"Was alcohol the reason San Francisco sucked for you?"

"It wouldn't have mattered if it was San Francisco or San Pedro. It would've been the same. Alcoholism is an illness. Otherwise I'd be ashamed of myself for being such a lousy soldier. I didn't know I couldn't control it. I didn't know about the *phenomenon of craving* that Bill Wilson figured out."

"I'm sure the alcoholic brain is just wired differently."

"If *you* have a shot glass of whisky, you sip it and sip it. You don't want to run out and buy a pint of it and start guzzling. I would. It triggers, what they called, the *phenomenon of craving*."

"How did alcoholism make you a lousy soldier?"

"Well, I didn't show up," Pops said with a chuckle.

"Where?"

"Work."

"In the kitchen?"

"I worked in the kitchen. But I worked in the post office, too."

"I didn't know that. Doing what?"

"Well, they had v-mail. They condensed the letter into a smaller package and we'd run it through the machine and make v-mail out of it. But I didn't know my ABCs, so I wasn't good at putting the letters in the right boxes."

"Illiterate?"

"Well, I was..." he didn't finish his thought.

"Mom said when she met you, you were reading the dictionary."

"I was."

"How'd you progress from not knowing your ABCs to being able to read the dictionary?"

"Honey, I probably still don't know my ABCs. Thanks for bringing that tobacco," he pivoted.

"What does that stuff do for you? Relax you or something?"

"I don't think you can explain it."

By this he means it's *cunning, baffling, powerful.*

"Does it change your thoughts or your head in some way?"

"All you can think about is the next drink," he said, pivoting back to booze. He must've forgotten we were talking about Copenhagen.

"It's the same with tobacco?"

"Same damn thing."

"What would happen if you weren't able to get this shit?"

"I'd be depressed and jumpy. This is powerful stuff," he said, holding the shiny silver can up.

"Were you chewing it all those years you were jogging?"

"Oh, yeah. I always chewed this."

"Since you were 7?"

"Something like that."

"Don't you think it's disgusting?"

"It's a terrible habit, I know," he said as he reached in the can with three fingers and pinched another gob into his mouth.

"I don't know what's worse, that shit or mom chain-smoking."

"Chain-smoking's a lot worse."

"Apparently, you're impervious," I told him. "That habit you've got there; it would've killed the average person already."

"I'm just lucky, I guess."

"How lucky are you to have me, Pops?"

"Really lucky, hon."

"Fuck the ABCs. You've got me."

"I'm really lucky."

"Would you like the know the most important thing I've learned so far in my life?" I wasn't going to let him not asking stop me from telling him.

"Well, of course."

"Let me cogitate on it for a second. You know where I first heard the word *cogitate*?"

"Where?"

"From you. You told me it meant 'to think deeply.'"

"It does."

"I know. You used to teach me vocabulary words during our ride to school every morning. Back when I went to Precious Blood during middle school."

This made Pops chuckle.

"How about a little more Elvis?" I pivoted.

Pops nodded his head in agreement, so I fished the remaining change out of my purse, got up from our booth and went over to the jukebox. I slipped my coins inside her once more and selected *It's Now or Never*.

"I'd have to say that the most important thing I've learned, and this might come as a shock to you, is that I don't need a relationship to be happy. I used to think I did. Or at least, the *phenomenon of craving* led me to believe it. I couldn't go a week without having someone. Yet, every time I did, which was often, I was miserable. Even when I had the best man any woman could ever hope to find, it wasn't enough. Just like you needed another drink, I needed another boyfriend.

It was madness.

Now, I only need myself. Shit, I'm all I've got. This idea was cliché before. Now, I'm living it. Being alone as long as I have forced me to cultivate the most important relationship of all—the one with myself. Who knew there was a universe inside of me? This vibrant inner world that I've been so fortunate to discover, rife with magic, is devoid of pain and without end. It can never be taken from me.

I read a lot of Joseph Campbell when Matthew and I were together. Before I went to NYU. Professor Campbell would often allude to this sacred place though at the time, it was pure abstraction. Now, it's my religion. I learned that until you have a meaningful relationship with yourself, your own heart and soul, you're not going to be prepared to have one with another. You've got to be your own first love."

After a moment of awkward silence, Pops nodded his head and took another sip of his coffee.

"There's one other thing I learned that's equally as important. Something Matthew taught me."

"What's that?"

"When you treat people who love you like shit, sooner or later they're going to walk away and never look back. That one's the hardest lesson of all. Believe me."

Pops stared blankly then took another sip of his coffee. I wanted more of response but he seemed distant. Half here, half who knows where. I wanted him to ask me some questions, to dig deeper, to show a scintilla of interest. He never did. It was the same with Kay. There's only so much they could ever give and it always left me craving more.

\*\*\*

## Monday, October 10, 1994

Dear Destiny,

I've decided to write you this letter. It may turn out to be the last one I send to you for quite some time. There's no guarantee those mysterious blue eyes have even touched these words thus far. Anyway, these have been a grueling five weeks. They've tested us as individuals and most importantly, they've tested our love for one another. Unfortunately, from where I'm sitting, I'm worried that at this hour we've failed. If we *have* failed, my insecurities are to blame.

You've said many times that being back there has given you clear sight into the whole matter of us and that you feel I've hurt you too deeply. Beyond repair. I know you want a life with me and want to work this all out somehow. And believe me, we can. As God is my witness, I want a life with you. I truly believe our love can conquer anything.

You've said numerous times that "love isn't enough." One of the many magical things about love is that it allows us to mend that which has been broken. Love allows us to forgive. I'm not dodging responsibility for anything. It's just that I know we can get through it. I've seen it in us, Destiny. Think about this: we've been together for almost a year and this problem has been at the center of our relationship the entire duration, and we've still made it.

I'm an asshole for what I've done to you, and you have every right to feel the way you do. All of your anger and animosity are justified. But just because you hate me for the way I've made you feel doesn't mean that we're through. See what I'm saying? You don't hate me. You're hurt. And you're back there in New York City just about as miserable as you can be questioning our relationship. Believe in us, Destiny. More importantly, believe in yourself.

I often wonder if your new friends ever give you the advice of forgiveness? Or have they said, "He's hurt you, Destiny, and because of that he's not worth a damn so drop that son of a bitch because you don't need him"? I'm defending myself because no one else will. I wonder why it is

144

that you haven't sought the advice of the people closest to you, the people that love and care about you most. People like your father and cousin Diana. They're the best people to talk to in a situation like this. They know they players. Believe it or not, your father only wants what's best for you and us. I told him everything yesterday. He thinks we can work it out.

I think you should continue with your therapy. It's free, why not take advantage of it? I think it would help alleviate a lot of the pain and anger you feel. You're going to find out when you start talking to someone that you're worth more than a million bucks. And the way that everyone, myself included, has made you feel is not the true story of Destiny Jones. I've seen so much beauty wrapped up inside you. Enough to last beyond this lifetime.

You're a special person, Destiny. It's time you learn this. Don't think I'm ducking the issues by being positive. Often, when I talk like this, you get angry and tell me that I'm simplifying everything to avoid taking responsibility. That's not true. People do change and I'm one of them. Despite what you say love *is* enough. How could I have possibly known then what I know now?

What I'm trying to say is that the past few months, especially September of 1994, have taught me so much. I'm no longer the person who hurt you. Lasting relationships are about people who hurt each other but find a way through it with the love they share. You seem to feel that I don't really love you. I think you feel that way when you're angry, but deep inside you know I do. You said on Saturday that our sicknesses don't coincide. What two people's ever do?

I hope this letter hasn't infuriated you. I've tried not to shift responsibility or place blame on your shoulders. I take full responsibility for my part in how you feel. Tomorrow's the first of many therapy sessions that are going to do me good. I'm beginning to understand exactly what I've done and why. I hope you can find it in your heart to forgive me for being ignorant and inexperienced.

I'm sorry if I haven't adhered to your request to leave you alone. If, by the time you've received and read this, you still feel you can't go on just let me know by mail and this will be the last letter. I haven't removed your bracelet from my wrist and never will. I love you, Destiny! I say a prayer for us every night that somehow, someday, you'll see the light.

Sincerely,
Matthew Ian

***

*"I've lost a lot of friends, as well as parents. A realization has come to me very, very keenly, however, that I haven't lost them. That moment when I was with them has an everlasting quality about it that is now still with me. What it gave me then is still with me, and there's a kind of intimation of immortality in that. There is a story of the Buddha, who encountered a woman who had just lost her son, and she was in great grief. The Buddha said, 'I suggest that you just ask around to meet somebody who has not lost a treasured child or husband or relative or friend.' Understanding the relationship of mortality to something in you that is transcendent of mortality is a difficult task."©*

**Saturday, February 18, 2017**

Dear Diary,

Today's Pops' 92nd birthday. He and I celebrated with some coffee and muffins in the little 1950s diner inside Windsor Court this afternoon. Our spot. Hard to believe he made it this far. He can't even believe it. The old man thinks I'm lying whenever I tell him his age.

"Destiny," he asked me again today, "how old am I?" as he took out a can of Copenhagen, cracked it open, and pinched a hearty gob into his mouth.

"Shit, Pops. I tell you every time. You're 92. Today's your birthday." I'm repulsed by the sight of that tobacco going into his mouth but since it's his birthday, I decided to keep mine shut.

"Are you sure?"

"I'm fucking positive."

"I'm 85," he said, dusting some crumbs off his chin.

"Seven years ago. You're 92 today."

"My God."

"Don't you believe me?"

"I don't know. It's hard to believe. How's Mike?" he asked, taking a slow shaky sip from his Styrofoam cup. A dribble of fresh tobacco already clung to the corner of his crinkled mouth. He may not know his ABCs, but Pops is able to chew snuff and drink coffee at the same time.

"Busy. He and Doug are always busy." I said, taking a bite of my blueberry muffin. Mike and his husband Doug are like my brothers. They're my most cherished gay friends ever since Richard committed suicide a few years back. I worked in Doug's store on Palm Canyon while I was getting my bachelor's degree at Cal State.

"Did you say I'm 92?"

"Today," I replied, waiting for him to call me a liar.

"Eighteenth of February?"

"Eighteenth of February."

"My God."

"Do you know what year it is, Pops?"

"It's uh...19 uh 17."

"No. You're on the right track, but it's not 1917."

"You sure? I think it is."

"We're in the middle of World War 1?"

"2017."

"There you go. Who's the President of the United States?"

Pops laughed then said, "I just heard that sonofabitch talk."

"What stupid shit did he say now?"

"He thinks the press ain't treatin' him fair."

"Where's this all going, Pops? You've seen a lot of presidents and watched a lot of history unfold. How's this going to end?"

"Well, you don't know with him. I think it'll go on just bullshit back and forth. He lies, you know. You can't have a president lying to the people." I couldn't help but laugh. Pops likes to lie, too. Or, should I say, deny the truth.

"I've been thinking about you, Pops, and all the fights you've been in and how hard you hit. Is it true that you just plain enjoy a good fight?"

"Well, I didn't take any guff off anybody."

"What happened to you in San Francisco when you were drunk in that bar and the AP, was it, the Army Police, beat the shit out of you with billy clubs?"

"I was fightin' 'em."

"How many?"

"Two."

"Why?"

"I was in the bar drinking and didn't want to go. They said, 'C'mon, we're taking you back to the base.' Somebody called and said 'Jim's at this bar drunk.' So instead of going with 'em, I just (he made a fist and mimicked punching someone). They pounded me over the head with billy clubs. The next day, my head was all swelled up. They took me into the commanding officer and he said, 'How come this little guy's all beat up?' And the sergeant said, 'You don't know this little guy when he's full of booze.' I was a drunk, hon. I didn't want to leave the saloon. But I've lived to be 85."

"92 goddamn it."

"Oh, that's right."

"How'd you do it?"

"I just kept breathing."

This made me laugh out loud.

"I'm afraid of getting old," I told him.

"It's better than the alternative."

"Death, you mean?"

"Damn straight."

He's said this before and it always puzzles me. For a man so full of history, philosophy, literature and life experience, my father seems to harbor a peculiar ambivalence about our ultimate destiny. One day he'll tell me he ain't afraid to die. That's he's going to die in his sleep. The very next day, getting old is "better than the alternative." Makes me wonder what the hell he really thinks. Does he even know? Does he just forget that he's not afraid? Realizing the moment's come for a pivot, I recalled something I'd been cogitating as of late. "I'm thinking about writing Matthew a letter."

"Mmm hmmm."

"Yeah." "What are you gonna say?"

"Probably 'hello.' And 'I miss you.' 'I'm sorry.' 'I've changed.' 'Thank you' and 'I still love you.'"

"Thank you for what? He left you."

"Exactly. Just like he should have. He should have left me a hell of a lot sooner, too. Like, when I was at NYU and hanging up on him all the time. I tortured that boy. I was toxic, imbalanced, abusive. He suffered way too long. Him leaving was the best thing that ever happened to me as painful as it's been. I want to thank him for helping make me a better person."

"If it'd make you feel better then you should do it."

"Eventually."

"But don't get your hopes up."

That's another thing about Pops that's bothered me since childhood. Never am I supposed to get "my hopes up" about *anything* I really want.

He's a perennial defeatist; the man who never followed his bliss. Whether it was about my acting career, my mom ever straightening out or anything else.

"Hopes up about what?"

"Hearin' from Matt."

"I can always count on you for a dose of optimism."

"I just don't wanna see you hurt again."

"The letter's not so that I can hear from him. I ain't going to hear from him. It's for me. It's so that I can sleep at night knowing I did my best to make amends. Don't you have to make amends? Isn't that what they teach you in A.A.? I don't know if you're aware or not but when I was at NYU those two and a half months, Matthew wrote me several exquisite love letters that I still possess. Whenever I feel down, I open the red box, randomly select one and start reading. His words continue to give me hope and strength. They're all I have left."

"If it's for your serenity, do it."

"I'm thinking about it."

"And if you ever do hear from Matt again since life is a mystery that way, just be his friend. Practice being his friend first. No hanky-panky. Just friends."

Was the old man actually giving me relationship advice? Was this the sound instruction I'd waited four decades to hear? Beside myself with joy, I felt this sudden turn of events was cause for celebration, as a surge of energy brought me to my feet.

"How about a birthday song, Pops? You love Chuck Berry, right?" Pops nodded in agreement. Borrowing some spare change from the old man since I'd run out, I got up from our booth and walked over to the jukebox once more. She had just the song I was thinking of. I slipped the coins inside her and selected Chuck Berry's 1955 classic: *Johnny Be Goode*. Released the year my mom graduated from San Dieguito High.

With the first riff of guitar another powerful urge overtook me. I flashed back to the summer of 1985 when Vicky Hewitt and I snuck out of the ABC Club and saw *Back to the Future* together at the Palm Desert Town Center. I had the biggest crush on Michael J. Fox at the time and begged her to take me. *Family Ties* was my favorite show.

Knowing it was likely one of the last birthdays I'd spend with the old man, I felt compelled to entertain him. The last time he saw me perform was when I played the voracious Ms. Finch in *Hazing the Monkey* at the Copperview Theater on Santa Monica Boulevard. Since I knew all the lyrics, I began lip-syncing the song, air guitar and all.

Within moments something remarkable happened. Residents of Windsor Court began gathering in the doorway of the diner. Ladies and gentleman who never appeared to have an expression on their withered faces showed signs of life for the first time. I too felt more alive. Ironic, considering I was in the last stop café. Most of these folks would die in that building. But at that moment in time, and by the looks on their faces that have seen it all, I was thoroughly entertaining them.

They gave me a warm round of applause when it was over. I hadn't heard that sound in a while.

I'm starting to appreciate mine and Pops' similarities. What he experienced with alcohol and tobacco is the same thing I experienced with sex and coffee. As dumb as my father was to punch a couple military cops, I was equally as dumb to do what I did to my beloved Matthew Ian.

The tender ghost that haunts me.

\*\*\*

**Friday, December 8, 2017**

Dear Diary,

It's the beginning of the calm before the storm. Yesterday was my last class of the first quarter in the teacher credential program. Two more to go.

I finally did it. I returned to Cal State San Bernardino in September to acquire my Single Subject Teaching Credential. Last time I set foot on their Palm Desert Campus was in 2011. Three months before Richard jumped off that Burbank overpass to his death. I was about to graduate with my B.A. in English Literature, and my obsession with professor David Marshall was in full-swing.

That's another story.

In a few short weeks, I begin the student teaching portion of the program at PDHS—my alma mater. Last time I set foot on that campus was grad night, 1992. Jemel (my first boyfriend) and I were there to celebrate everyone's graduation: Lindsey, Carrie, Jenica, Beau, Sheilagh, Teresa, Windy, Lynn, Kim, Tiff, et al. The thought of student teaching there makes me want to piss my pants, but I'm determined. I've wasted enough time settling for less than I deserve—shitty jobs, shitty friends, shitty men. Fuck it. After years of pulling shots for hipster scum at Koffee, I had a decision to make: either grow a pair and get this done or pull shots for hipster scum ad infinitum. The horrifying latter was not an option.

Today was a great day. I got to spend it with Stephen and Maria Alaina in La Quinta. They want to move to Brazil where Stephen can focus on *Scalar Heart Connection®* and Maria Alaina can write poetry, study astrology and tend to the garden. I can't bear the thought of losing them. You don't find friends like them every day. I can't be selfish either. The walls are metaphorically closing in on them here. Maria Alaina said she can literally hear her neighbor fart inside of his house sometimes when she's on her patio.

"I'd kill myself," I said, suddenly overcome with the urge to confess something to her. "You guys are irreplaceable. You cannot be replaced."

"Aww, Destino!"

We've been friends for seven years. I met Maria Alaina in Nan Tynberg's literary theory class at Cal State. She and her husband Stephen are the high-end version of Tom and Cynthia. Tom was an insurance adjuster; Stephen paints, writes, and cogitates Jung. Cynthia was addicted to cocaine and pills; Maria Alaina is vegan with the same passion for astrology as I possess.

When I visited her today, she had some primo ganja for us to smoke. A friend of hers owns an organic pot farm in Humboldt, so she always has the very best. As we sat on her patio while Stephen was inside, Maria Alaina took a hit from her tiny glass pipe, exhaled, passed it to me then declared, "It's 11:11 and we're here talking. Are we in synchronicity or what?"

This made me laugh. Her Chilean accent and quirky grammar make what she says funny to me sometimes. *All* the time? Often.

"I totally have been," I said.

"I've been like this all day, in this vibration, synchronicity."

"Last week, I dreamt that I was telling somebody about synchronicities that I've experienced. The very next day, I found myself in class telling a girl about synchronicities and the fact that I'd just dreamt about telling someone about synchronicities."

"I love it. It's like synchronicity within synchronicities."

"Right?"

"Brilliant. So, what do my cards say right now?"

By "cards" she meant her Destiny Cards. Ironic, I know. I opened my heavily worn copy of Robert Lee Camp's book of the same title, my bible ever since discovering the fascinating *Science of the Cards* system circa 2003, shortly after I moved back to the desert. When doing card readings, I look first to the yearly long-range card for a clue as to what the client might expect during that particular year of their life. It's like their yearly theme. "It looks like you have the nine of spades long-range this year."

"What is this nine of spades?"

"It's one of the traditional cards of death. Like the ace of spades. But unlike the ace of spades which can broadly mean a 'transformation,' the nine of spades tends to speak of actual physical death. You just experienced major death. Your grandma Mutti burns up in a fire and then your father dies suddenly. That's heavy shit. Nine of spades. On a more fundamental level it's about endings. Graduations. It's a powerful, universal card signaling that it's time to let go of something that's no longer doing you any good. And let go you must or else."

"I let go of my uterus."

"Right. Your surgery."

"Oui."

"That's a death of sorts. Certainly an ending."

"I see it like an ancestral ending. No more of this myomas passed on from women to women from abortions or lost children or whatever."

"Wait. Say that again." The word "abortion" got my attention.

"Myomas."

"What is that?"

"Problems in the uterus that reflect inherited patterns of losses of children through abortions, natural abortions, losses of kids. They form like a cyst."

"I've never heard of this. *Myomas.*"

"Have you had an abortion?"

"Regrettably, yes. Will I get myomas?"

"Depends on your ancestral karma."

The subject of abortions gives me anxiety so I quickly pivoted. The old man would be proud. "Are you guys really moving to Brazil?"

"Destino, you can visit anytime. We're done here."

I chuckled. Probably to conceal the pain I felt. "That's an ending, a graduation. It's also very five of spades of you. That's your second card."

"My second card?"

"Your Planetary Ruling Card. Being a Libra, you're ruled by Venus, and your Venus card is the five of spades—*The Wanderer.* You *are* the wanderer, aren't you?"

154

"I just love the fucking unknown."

"That statement sounds more like your ace of spades karma card talking. It represents the unknown more than the five of spades does, though they're similar being of the same suit. What's my chart saying these days? Will I survive student teaching?"

Maria Alaina brought her focus to her laptop and pulled up my astrological chart. She gazed at it a long time. "For you, comes a change in your career."

"I fucking hope so."

"Oh yeah."

"Shit, I haven't had any career. Teaching will be the career."

"Because you've been in Pisces."

My thoughts instantly trail off to Matthew, a Pisces.

"Uranus in Pisces. Once Uranus enters full force back you'll feel more directional, more clarity."

"What else do you see?" I inched to the edge of my seat as she looked closely at my chart again.

"You find your man. You get married actually."

"I get married?"

"You get married but it's like…"

"To who and when?"

"You have some man but it's like an older time for you, and it's very good, very satisfying."

"What do you mean? When *I'm* older?"

"You get married in an older time because you have Jupiter in the 7th house but it's in Capricorn ruled by Saturn—the father of time. I would say in your 50s, in the middle of 50s. Actually, it's like a…" She paused for a long time appearing to connect aspects in my chart. "…almost like a partner in some project. He's a partner in some project of communication that's out

155

of this plane. Almost a dialogue between men and women. You just need to get over whatever wound you bring from your ancestors. A wound that's related to men."

"There've been a few."

"One man in particular. You get stuck in your mind with that and it holds you back from your real experiencing, your growth, your potential, your healing, your talents, your lessons in this world, this lifetime, which all has to do with your spiritual growth. So get over your wound and you will transform and grow, and get to your destiny."

We both laughed at the intentional irony.

"The wound is with men, and it's passed through generations forever on your women's side," she repeated.

"But what is it? This wound."

"It has to do with feeling overwhelmed and confused on who they are; not having a place—especially an intellectual place—within the male dominated world. Not recognized for their intellect. You came from a lineage of women who liked to exercise their intellect but were pushed down for it by men. The men, out of their own insecurity, filled them with doubt. That's the wound. And they don't know what to do with it for generations. So, they have to eat their thoughts. Because they can't speak it. Maybe they have hidden writing but if they wrote certain things they might have been ridiculed or even killed. You see all the wounds there? Once you get over that—your doubt—you move into your spiritual world which is being fully in touch with your emotions. Don't stop your creative process. Are you making a list?"

"I have a list. What kind of list do you want?"

"A very specific list like…*you want a man and...*"

The first item on this hypothetical list was funny to me.

"I'm just fine with my dogs and cat."

"So now that you're not looking, bang! Someone will show up."

"I have no idea. I just realize more and more how much I enjoy my pets. How much I love them, and this is ok."

"But work will bring you a man regardless."

We suddenly heard a door open.

"Is that Stephen?" Maria Alaina asked.

"I thought I heard the door."

"He might bring us a coffee."

"Are you drinking coffee?" I asked, delighted. "Like a real coffee? Oh my God."

Stephen appeared holding two small cups.

"Are you bringing us coffee?" she asked him.

"I'd bring donuts but I don't have any," said Stephen as he sat our steaming coffees onto the patio table. The midday sun shone brightly in the frothy crema.

"Thank you, thank you" I said, joyfully taking one of the cups. I love coffee, it's no secret. But what I love even more is coffee paired with organic Humboldt herb. Talk about the perfect combo. Sativa and caffeine. A beautiful, beautiful thing.

"It's strong," he told us before departing back inside.

"I didn't realize you guys were drinking coffee. This is great."

"A cup here and there."

"I can't give up coffee. I've already given up so much."

"I don't drink it every day. I'd be wired," said Maria Alaina.

"I need it every day. It's how I keep on truckin.'" My thoughts trailed back off to Matthew once more. I realized that I'd just uttered a common phrase of his. One that I don't recall uttering before.

"Anyway," Maria Alaina pivoted back to our earlier discussion. "You can choose if you don't want to marry. But the proposal should be in your 50s."

"How do you know this?"

"Saturn. It's right here," she points to what she's looking at in my chart. "And when it touches here, your 7th house, it means a contract. How's your father by the way?"

"He's fine. But he has COPD."

"My god, how many years is he now? 98?"

"In February he'll be 93."

"Oh, 93? Ah, he's still young."

"He's still young?"

"He's still young."

"How will I know when the end is truly near?"

"When will be his time to go? Remember the *Synchronicity Symposium*? Dr. Tarnas said that synchronicities increase around births and deaths."

"So I need to be on the lookout for synchronicity?"

"Yes, and it's all right here in your chart. Look at how magical that is. You see?" She took her righthand index finger and outlined the grand air trine I have between my Sun/Saturn, Jupiter and Uranus. She then took her finger and traced Saturn's ultimate move from my fifth to seventh house.

"Why does Saturn signify a marriage?" I asked her.

"Saturn is your contract; when you sign papers. Natal Jupiter there is your happiness. And it's all in the house of partnerships."

"Does that give any indication of the astrological sign of this mythical person? Or any other information about them?"

"It gave me the impression that he's another teacher; a very Sagittario person. He's a mixture between Sagittario and Capricorn. But he has a spin with the mind; quite an intelligent person. Maybe he's a history teacher. A writer for sure, beautiful writer, but he has an off-spin just like you do. So you guys hit it at that level."

"A history teacher. No shit? And a writer? I'm listening." I couldn't be any more captivated by the delicious clues my dear friend was offering. It was a miracle I remained in my seat.

***

**Sunday, October 30, 1994**

Love of My Life,

Happy Anniversary! I can't say it's been a very good one for me. This whole weekend's been shitty to tell you the truth. My dad went back into the hospital today. His chest has been congested and he's had trouble breathing. He looks worse this time around. Remember how he was when we picked him up from Eisenhower last year? Strong, confident and all. This time he looks frightened. I think he feels alone. Mark and Luke are bad company. They just sit and watch MTV all day, assuming someone else will do whatever has to be done.

I'm sorry if I upset you on the phone last night. I didn't mean to. What I was trying to say before you hung up on me is that you're growing up. You're responsible for yourself now. That's why there's so much pain. Growing up is painful. That's what they failed to teach us in school. And in order to grow up you have to reconcile your mother and father, and forgive them.

Think of all this as just the beginning. You and only you are responsible for what happens from here on out. Before, you were dependent on your parents and your mom let you down in a big way. She prioritized herself over you every time. How devastating for a sweet little girl. But if you just open up, let me in and allow yourself to feel the love of others, all that pain will turn into strength and wisdom.

When you talk about suicide it really scares me. Look at Kurt Cobain. In one of his songs he sings, "Teenage angst has paid off well, now I'm bored and old." He took his life at 27 when he had a wife who loved him and a baby daughter. What a waste! Nothing's that bad, Destiny. Look for the good and the beauty in things. It's there. I feel like that's something you really struggle with. Why? Why are you so pessimistic? Remember what Joseph Campbell said in "The Journey Inward" chapter:

*"Ramakrishna once said that if all you think of are your sins, then you are a sinner. And when I read that, I thought of my boyhood, going to confession on Saturdays, meditating on all the little sins that I had committed during the week. Now I think one should go and say, 'Bless me, Father, for I have been great, these are the good things I have done this week.' Identify your notion of yourself with the positive, rather than with the negative."* ©

Think of everything through that lens. Think positively. That's what I want you to earnestly practice starting today. Right this minute. There's no time to waste. Practice seeing yourself *as you are* and your life *as it is* in a positive light.

Can't you see all that pain comes from outside yourself? You've harbored it but it's not your fault. You've been victimized. We all have to a certain degree. Don't blame yourself, just let it out. I can tell that you need to. I can tell you've been holding something inside of you far too long. Some ineffable wound inflicted long before me, Phil, or Jemel ever entered the picture. You need to cry, Destiny. Cry with me. Cry on my shoulder. Cry in my arms. There's nothing I want more in this world than to see your pain disappear. Please read *The Neverending Story*. After you read that I want you to read Herman Hesse's *Demian*. You should see yourself in both of these books.

Not to change the subject or anything but...

My dick is hard for you right now. It's literally aching and oozing. When you told me you're not going to wear panties anymore it really turned me on. I can't stop thinking about it. Sexual thoughts of you are relentless and overwhelming. My dick is constantly hard. I've already masturbated twice today and fear I may have to do it until my palms bleed. I'm going fucking crazy without you!

That first night is going to be wonderful. Wear one of your little sheer dresses with no bra. Your luscious tits drive me wild. I want to lie on my back while you straddle my face and suck my cock. I love how wet you get when my dick is in your mouth. When you can't take it anymore and need me inside of you, I want you to spin around, put your palms on my bare chest and slide down every inch of me nice and slow—on your terms. The thought of that moment consumes me. And after almost three months your pussy should be super tight again, a pleasure that can't be measured.

Once I'm all the way in and can feel your cervix, I want you to sit up straight so I can see the shape of your breasts through your dress and watch your nipples get hard as you slowly start to ride me, rocking your hips back and forth as I grip them, moaning loudly like always. And since we both know how much you love riding my big dick, it won't be long before those moans become screams, that pussy starts to flutter, and squeeze, and grip me tighter and tighter until a warm rush of our mutual ecstasy spills out everywhere.

I just came my brains out again. I couldn't help myself.

Never wonder about the depth of my devotion to you. I'll do anything you tell me to. Just let me in. Let me love you, Destiny Jones. I won't allow anyone to hurt you ever again. No one's going to laugh at your picture around me. I'm so proud that you're my woman. I can't wait to show you starting on December 22$^{nd}$.


Your friend and lover,
Matthew Ian


***

*"You know, we have a tremendous amount of information about the subject, but there is a place where the information stops. And until you have writing, you don't know what people were thinking. All you have are significant remains of one kind or another. You can extrapolate backward, but that is dangerous. However, we do know that burials always involve the idea of the continued life beyond the visible one, of a plane of being that is behind the visible one to which we have to relate. I would say that is the basic theme of all mythology—that there is an invisible plane supporting the visible one. Burials suggest that my friend has died, and that he survives."©*

## Friday, December 22, 2017

Dear Diary,

Today's the day I've been anxiously awaiting my entire life. 44 ½ years. It's the morning of December 22, 2017. I just got off the phone with the head nurse at Windsor Court who tearfully informed me that my father James has passed away. He didn't get up for breakfast this morning and when the caregivers checked on him, he was gone. I can't believe it. I just saw him. I brought him two cans of tobacco yesterday.

The nurse also informed me there'd been an incident.

"What kind of incident?" My heart fluttered as I grasped the handle of the refrigerator with my free hand to keep from falling. During the election, Pops punched an old man in the face during supper in the "mess hall" (his term) for allegedly calling Hillary Clinton a "bitch." Afterward, the director guy told me that if he hits anyone else they'll have to call the police. I knew it was only a matter of time.

"He got up in the middle of the night and started hitting Olaf."

"Oh shit."

"So we separated them."

"Oh my God," I gripped the refrigerator handle a little tighter.

"Sometime before dawn your dad returned to his room, went to sleep and never woke up."

*Lucky for him he never woke up* was my first thought. As if I'm not shocked enough the old man's a corpse, she has to go and tell me his final act on this beautiful earth was battery of that sweet old barber he roomed with.

I wish she hadn't.

"Is Olaf ok?"

"He's fine. I don't think he knew what was happening."

"I'm sorry. Tell him I'm so sorry. Pops beat my ass all the time when I was little, so I know how he feels. I'll make arrangements immediately."

"I'm sorry for your loss. Your dad was a sweet man."

"Thank you." I sat my phone down on the white tile counter and swung my right hand around to join the left one clinging to the fridge handle. The tile floor felt colder than ever beneath my bare feet. Had it always been this cold? Had my house always felt this empty? This quiet? This serene? I couldn't recall.

Today's the day, as a vulnerable child and insecure young adult, I was convinced would send me crashing to the ground. But thanks to my vintage 2001 General Electric refrigerator, that didn't happen. Part of me was convinced the old man would never die; that he couldn't die. I imagined death herself trembled to take him.

Thank God I stopped by to see him yesterday. Although I didn't say a proper goodbye. I was in a hurry to get to Stephen and Maria Alaina's for our solstice celebration. If I'd have known that was going to be it, I wouldn't have rushed out. I would've uttered some parting words of appreciation. Would a, could a, should a. It's done.

Rather than entertain this futile line of thought too long, I unclasped my rigid grip, walked over to my coffee maker and started brewing another pot of Trader Joe's medium roast arabica instead.

### *Eight hours later...*

Maria Alaina and Taylor just left. They were here for about three hours. I never dreamt I'd be so blessed to have such lovely ladies by my side on this momentous day. Maria Alaina got here first, around noon. We wasted no time getting down to our favorite business: smoking, talking and drinking kombucha.

"These days are charged with death," Maria Alaina declared as she poured a purple glass of GT's Divine Grape that she'd procured between her house and mine. "These last couple of days my mom went to my grandmother's place."

"That burned down?"

"Yeah. So I was already feeling this heaviness in my chest. Then yesterday I was all teary about my dad. I've been feeling these last few days really heavy around death, but I didn't know what was coming."

"Death was coming," I said. "Death always comes to me in the wintertime. My mom died during winter. At three o'clock in the morning on January 1, 1999."

"January first?"

"1999," I repeated, choking back baby tears by the third nine. "Another cold Friday morning. A year before she died, that ex-boyfriend I always talk about..."

"Mateo."

"Who I desperately loved but couldn't handle left me after 4 ½ painful years. In the wintertime. It was after the two of them died, literally and figuratively, that..." I lost my train of thought.

"That?"

I found it again. "I fell apart. Things fell apart around me and so did I. Six months later I started drinking and doing drugs. And not the ganja either. Back then I liked the bad shit. Ecstasy. Cocaine..."

"You lost yourself."

164

"And I was left with old man Jones."

"I'm going to change something in your language," Maria Alaina swiftly interjected, appearing to take issue with my choice of words. "*I was left*. In these words you put yourself as a victim. I know you don't want to be that. So you can say: *I chose to stay here with my dad*. Because you always have a choice. What's your father's name again?"

"James. But everyone calls him Jim."

"James," she said sweetly as her attention moved to the large Buddhist icon I'd placed on my kitchen counter before she arrived. "Maybe there with Buddha we can put a picture of James. Do you have a picture of your dad?"

Without a word I jumped up and ran to the master bedroom, his old room, and returned with an 8x10 black and white silver-framed portrait of him that had been gathering dust in the closet.

"He's maybe 21 here."

"Fuck, he's adorable. Put him next to Buddha. Not forever but for a few weeks while you go through a mourning process. You gonna see him, you gonna talk to him, you gonna cry. You've got to go through the process."

"See, that's what I didn't do when my mom died. I didn't cry at all. I was numb. My friends were like, 'Destiny, we're worried about you. Your mother just died and you seem unfazed.'"

"You know that's no good."

"Same thing with Matthew. Numb. Nothing. Denial."

"Okay, so with James you gonna let the tears roll. You gonna look at his picture, and talk to him, and they come out. They come in waves. It's called 'mourning.'"

"I've never really done that. Not enough anyway."

"No? Then it's time. It's very healthy to grieve and feel sad."

In the middle of her speech *Smart Cremation* called. I paused her so that I could take their call in the bathroom. "They've already got him," I said, reemerging a minute later. "I was worried that I was going to get in trouble for what he did to Olaf."

"Remember, we don't have control of how they die or the karma involved with other people. We just have to go through the process."

There was something about her serene Libran voice, her delightful Chilean accent, her mere presence that comforted me. I'll never forget the time she told me about the blue flame. She'd dreamt about an intense blue flame flickering out of a tiny hole in the ground. Whenever she looked at it, she was paralyzed with fear. Before she awoke, it was revealed to her what the blue flame was—her feminine power. She claims not to remember the dream. But I do.

"It's just weird because when they die you're left with a doubt," Maria Alaina continued. "But don't feed it. It's like with Mutti. We don't know if the fire at her place was intentional, so we don't feed that thought. Or with my dad. If I really begin to investigate why he died; why he was having mini-strokes…you see? He was taking a drug, a vasoconstrictor. You know what that means? It's like constricting the blood tubes. He was having issues with peeing too much and this drug was helping with not peeing. If I were to really look into that, I could find all sorts of bad things. But I don't. What is the solution when you have a doubt?"

"Don't feed it said the seven of clubs."

"What is this card?"

"*Spiritual Knowledge* and transforming negative thinking."

"Exactly. Because it's not going to change the fact that he is dead; that he is in another plane with your mom. My dad is with his mom and dad. Mutti's up there, too. You just have to see that they're on a different plane now. And that they're here, too. He might come and say goodnight to you in your dreams."

"I told him to send me lots of playing cards."

"Ok, so get his card and place it on our altar." I spun around in my chair, grabbed the black Bicycle Guardian deck that Jeff (the oversexed anti-Christ I met online) gave me that was sitting on a table near the entryway, shuffled through it until I found the seven of diamonds—the *Magical Money* card and handed it to her.

"One of the reasons that we do this—the altar—is so he can understand that he is in another plane now; so that he doesn't get stuck. That's why we light the candles, so he goes toward the light. I'm sure the loss of his wife has been terrible for him. No?"

Her question made me laugh out loud. "Kay?"

"Is that your mom?"

"Yeah."

"Yeah, Kay."

"No."

"Oh?"

"You mean her death?"

"Yeah."

"I never saw any indication of that."

"So it was love and hate?"

I was unable to answer her as I had little insight into the peculiar relationship of my parents. People who never slept in the same bed and divorced when I was nine. When my mom was homeless around the time I was at NYU, Pops let her come live with him though it didn't last long. She fucked it up like she always did.

"Sometimes people don't know how to show love," Maria Alaina said. "He didn't know how to show love. But we understand that and we forgive him. You can say that to him: *Dad, I understand that you didn't know how to show love.*"

Fighting the urge to laugh out of pure discomfort, I repeated the phrase anyway. "Dad, I understand that you didn't know how to show love." The impulse to laugh was merely a defense against the intense feeling of pity that swelled up in my chest as I uttered the words. It wasn't just Jim who didn't know how to show love. Neither did Kay. Suffice to say, I received no demonstrable love from either of them when I was little.

"Why do you think he wasn't able to show you love? Or anyone for that matter?" Maria Alaina asked.

"Nobody taught him."

"Because they didn't know themselves."

"But how can that be?"

"Wasn't he the older one?"

"First born of five. Right before the Great Depression."

"So his mother got pregnant and it was in the worst condition to be pregnant at that time. Then, you expect a lot from the older one. There's always a difference in the treatment of the first child, the second, third, and so forth. And if parents don't know any better they beat their kids, and the kids rebel, and they beat more," she said with a scratchy voice. "I need tea."

"My entire childhood was a series of brutal beatings."

"You see. But you are going to break that ancestral pattern." With that, she got up from my dining room table to make herself some chamomile tea in the kitchen.

By the time the kettle was boiling, Taylor arrived bearing fragrant flowers and a vibrant green salad. "I got these flowers because they smell so good," she said, handing them to me when I greeted her at the door. I met sweet Taylor, like Stephen, through Maria Alaina.

"Oh they do, they do," said Maria Alaina from the kitchen. "I can smell them all the way over here." At once, the room fell deathly quiet. Unable to bear an awkward silence, I started firing off the questions. This one, directed at Taylor.

"Is it weird to be around somebody who just lost a loved one?"

"No. I just didn't know what to expect."

I proceeded to tell her about how my father allegedly beat on his roommate hours before he died. "I'm just upset that his dying act was hitting someone," I told the girls.

"Maybe he was fighting death," Taylor suggested.

"That's exactly what I thought," I said.

"It's like that poem: *Do Not Go Gentle Into that Good Night*. It says, *'And you, my father, there on the sad height. Curse, bless, me now with your fierce tears, I pray. Do not go gentle into that good night. Rage, rage against the dying of the light.'* It's urging you to live your life to the fullest with every breath until the bitter end."

"What kind of music did your dad like?" asked Maria Alaina.

"Country western. Oldies but goodies."

"You know what I did when my father died?" she continued. "I played a heart-wrenching song called *Mi Viejo*. Old man, my dear old man. It's about a young man whose father was about to pass. All my life, because I live far away from my dad, that song was always hard for me to hear. The day he died, I played it and just sing with it and cry with it. I feel the deepest of emotions."

"It's when we don't that problems arise." As soon as the words left my lips the irony they oozed dripped all over me. My thoughts quickly turned to Matthew as they so often did. I realized with great clarity that I've never had that special cry in his honor. Instead, I relegated his tragic death to the back of my mind with the hope it was but a temporary hell, and that someday he'd be resurrected like Christ; my sins washed away.

"It was hard to go to those deep dark places with people," Maria Alaina continued. "That's why, when I came back after Mutti and my dad died, I needed time alone so I can just cry my head off. I can't even have Stephen around because he worries. I just need to live this intensity because I know I'll be out of it soon."

"I finally did that with my mother," I said. "Six years after she died. There's a book called *Motherless Daughters*. The last time I did drugs, I

169

started reading it after being up all night in my bedroom. I wept and wailed on a level like never before. It was orgasmic. The next day, I checked myself into rehab at the ABC Cub for the second time and never touched that shit again. I'd finally been cleansed. My own tears had cleansed me."

"I don't want to get all psychoanalytic or anything," said Taylor, "but my therapist always tells me that when we have addictions we're actually trying to replace significant relationships. Usually abusive or neglectful parents. I feel like you made that connection on your own."

"Exactly," said Maria Alaina. "When we lose our father we tend to smoke. And then the smoking addiction is passed on."

Not ironically, both of us had smoked profusely after she arrived.

"My mother chain-smoked Winstons day and night, and had no relationship with her birth father," I said. "Then her step father started having sex with her when she was four. Her alcoholic mother caught him in the act but didn't do anything to stop it. That's why Kay's dead right now. I should have a mother. But she's dead, too. She'd been dying since the day I was born."

"Oh my goodness," the girls said in unison before I even finished my last sentence. The house fell deathly quiet again. The chirping of desert birds gathered on green succulents outside made their way in for a good minute.

Then, Maria Alaina seemed to have a revelation.

"Wait, I have something Stephen wrote about addiction. It's in the car." She sat her cup of tea on the counter, grabbed her keys from her bag, went outside to her blue 4Runner named Azula and returned with a spiral notebook. "This is something Stephen is working on." She sat down at my dining room table in between Taylor and I, opened the purple notebook and began reading:

*"It is the separation from mother that is at the heart of addiction. And that separation from mother is only a mirror image of our Grand Separation from the Divine. Therefore, we are all born into the feeling of being rejected by God. We attempt to replace this feeling of rejection and emptiness with the love of mother, father, family, friends, coworkers, etc. But in the end, these can never replace the Divine Love that is the foundation of who we are at the level of Soul. It is the story of the Prodigal Son who wanted to see the world and so he left his Father's House to experience the world (physical existence). The Father waits patiently for the son to learn that only his home in the Divine Palace will make him truly happy. In the meantime, we attempt to fill that which can never be filled with alcohol, nicotine, drugs, sex..."*

"Coffee!" I exclaimed.

*"…. anything that will numb our mind to the pain of separation from the Divine. In Scalar Heart Connection ®, I find that the client has always lost a connection to the Divine, their Higher Self, Soul, etc. Ultimately, the Divine activates the archetype of emptiness in order to motivate us towards Love of Soul and away from love of the world. It is actually a blessing to be touched in this way by the finger of God. Painful, yes, but when do human beings ever change without the motivation of pain?*

*I also find in my clients that a cigarette or smoking addiction is related to issues with father. The lungs are connected to the element of metal, and metal is associated with father. Inhaling nicotine is an attempt to fill a void left by an absent father. Carl Jung considered issues with father to be issues with the Divine Father. We can't forget that cultivating a connection or relationship with the Divine is a lifelong endeavor.*

*In the meantime, we can start by practicing gratitude. To be grateful that we were given a life and an opportunity to see the stars, trees, oceans, children's smiles, etc. We can also take a pause from our feelings towards our mother and consider that she, too, was a product of her experiences with her mother. At some point, we learn to rise above 'motherness' and become the child of the Universe. We can cultivate this by turning our*

*attention towards helping others with an open, grateful, and joyful heart."*
*—© Stephen L.*

"Talk about synchronicity," I said.

### *The next morning...*

You'll never believe what happened last night. After the girls left and I wrote my last word here, Taylor texted to tell me to be sure and look up to the sky as there was an exquisite desert sunset closing out the eventful day. By the time I made it to my double-paned window, the sunset was fast receding into the western twilight behind Mount San Jacinto.

With a sigh, I closed this diary, grabbed my purse, went into the garage, got into my car and proceed to drive toward Doug and Mike's house five minutes down the road. Def Leppard's 1987 classic, *Hysteria*, was fortuitously on deck and track two—*Rocket*—had just begun.

*Of hopeless night / will you love me?*

I rolled down my street and turned the corner onto Mission Lakes Boulevard toward the boys' house. All of sudden, high in the darkening blue sky, a bright white light careened across the horizon in unison with the song.

*White lights, strange city, mad music all around*
*Midnight, street magic, crazy people, crazy sound*

"What the fuck?" was all I could muster as I watched it stop then slowly start to expand across pink and lavender clouds. There's something spinning around inside it. "What the fuck is *that*?"

*Jack Flash, Rocket Man, Sergeant Pepper and the band*
*Ziggy, Bennie and the Jets*
*Take a rocket, we just gotta fly*
*I can take you through the center of the dark*
*We're gonna fly (on a collision course to crash into my heart)*
*I will be your, I will be your, I'll be your*

172

*Rocket, yeah, satellite of love* ©

There were no other words. I hadn't a clue what I was looking at. There was no prior knowledge from which to draw. Was it a meteorite? Maybe. Were we being attacked by North Korea? Russia? I started fumbling for my cellphone which is somewhere in my purse on the passenger seat. The cars in front of me started pulling over one by one as I inched past them never taking my eyes off the spectacle in the sky. I wanted to record it, lest no one believe me, as whatever it was continued to expand against the Milky Way.

I needed air, so I pulled the car over, flung open the door and stepped outside. The others who'd pulled over had stepped outside too and had their cellphones heavenward, doing what I had wanted to before I needed air. As a cool desert zephyr swirled around me, my mind was flooded with a thousand images; a kaleidoscope of memories of love's labour's lost. Random scenes from my life flickered behind my eyes in tableau. I saw myself talking to Bret Michaels, Bobby Dall and Tommy Lee when I was with Dominic.

Which reminded me, I had another classic 80s metal album in the back seat. Cinderella's *Long Cold Winter* from 1988. Released at the end of my freshman year. The good old days. I got back inside my Honda, ejected *Hysteria,* put Cinderella in and clicked forward to track three: *Don't Know What You've Got (till it's Gone).*

The anthem of my broken heart.

Every time I hear this song, I flash back to the 10th grade sitting in my room in the tiny apartment I shared with Kay in Palm Desert. This cassette is blaring on my vintage late '80s stereo as I do homework in my daybed. How I long for that innocent time!

As the music started to play the tears started to roll. I fumbled my glasses off my face, wiping away salty drops with the top of my wrist.

> *I can't tell you baby what went wrong*
> *I can't make you feel what you felt so long ago*
> *I'll let it show*

*I can't give you back what's been hurt*
*Heartaches come and go and all that's left are the words*
*I can't let go*

*If we take some time to think it over baby*
*Take some time, let me know*
*If you really want to go*

It was as if everything I'd never cried about was with me now in the street. Desert birds gathered on surrounding succulents and began their enchanting chorus. It felt like they were singing to me. Then came the epiphany: *You can't go back.*

*Don't know what you got till it's gone*
*Don't know what it is I did so wrong*
*Now I know what I got*

It was that subtle voice that often speaks to me inside my head: *You can only go forward.*

*It's just this song*
*And it ain't easy to get back*
*Takes so long©*

*Let go and move forward in faith.* With what felt like a direct transmission from my soul penetrating me right there on Mission Lakes Boulevard, I turned around, placed both palms open on the hood of my car and hung my weary head. Not caring who might see or what they might think, I cried like never before until the song faded with the dying light six minutes later.

It was revealed in the *Washington Post* this morning that the strange sight in last night's sky wasn't an attack after all. It was a SpaceX Falcon 9 rocket launch from Vandenberg Air Force Base. My father's weary soul, presumably on board.

What an incredible coincidence!

174

\*\*\*

**Saturday, November 5, 1994**

Dear Destiny,

Where are you? At work? In your room? Have you heard my messages? What is happening? I don't know what's wrong or how you're feeling. I'm going out of my mind. How much more pain am I going to have to endure? Are you still resentful and angry at me for what's in the past? What have I done lately?

Nothing's happening here in Palm Desert except for the gut-wrenching anticipation of December 22, 1994. Your message on my machine today was weird. I've listened to it twice now and I'm convinced that you're hiding something from me. What is it? What is happening or has happened? You said that you didn't hang up on me last night but that the line just disconnected. Why was it busy for five minutes afterward? Why didn't you call me right back? Were you in the room to hear the three messages I left on your machine right after? If you were there, why didn't you pick up the phone?

You were acting strange last night, too. You weren't talkative. You've been acting strange since last Sunday. You've been distant. What's happening back there? Your message said that we can't talk until Thursday. I find time in my schedule to talk to you. Shit, I've paid for most of our conversations thus far. What the fuck?

I'm fucking angry because this is complete bullshit. You think you're under pressure? Well so am I. How the hell do you think it makes me feel to have the woman I love and cherish more than anything fucking with my mind while my father's in the hospital and my brothers are up to no good? All the while I'm trying to be a good brother and take some sort of responsibility for them. All the while I'm loaded down with school work. I always find time for you. I take an hour out of almost every day to write to you.

I have to admit that last night right before our conversation came to an end it sounded as if you had something to say or confess. We were talking about *Oleanna* and I said, "Hello, Destiny, are you there?" Nothing. Then I heard a single, "Matthew..." and then silence. I remember it all perfectly. I called right back—busy. What happened? Did you set the phone down or something? Why didn't you call me back? For some reason you didn't want to talk to me and that hurts.

I have to say that for the first time in over a year I'm really pissed off at you. I mean, *fucking pissed*. This is bullshit. We can't talk until Thursday? Why? Why are you running from me? What's going on? What did Christina say to you at dinner? Or did you even go out with Christina? You were an hour late and hardly apologized. How would you feel if you planned your whole day around a telephone call and the person you love flaked on you?

After I left the first message I was hit with an overwhelming sense that something's really wrong; that there's someone else. I have to be honest, after I left that message a voice went off in my head. I actually said it out loud, "She's cheating on me!" Of course, this is my greatest fear and the worst possible thing that could happen. You've been talking about infidelity a lot lately. The other day you asked me out of nowhere if I'd cheated on you and if I had, would I tell you. Just because you had some flash at work you questioned my devotion to you. When I tell you that that hurt my feelings, you reply, "Well, I'm just worried because of my psychic thing." What kind of thing is that to say?

Why is it that your roommate Erin's fucked up life has some bearing on ours? I asked you this question in an earlier letter and never got a response. I'm not with someone else. Are you? I'm really worried. You haven't been yourself and I'm concerned as to why. Are people continuing to pump bullshit doubts into your head? How is it affecting you? What is happening? I just want to talk. I hope this letter hasn't hurt your feelings. I'm in a lot of pain right now. Not talking to you under these circumstances is painful enough let alone having to live with the chaos and hell I live with every day here. I hope you can see things from my perspective someday soon. I know I've faltered at times and that I've hurt you, but I've also been an excellent, compassionate, devoted, and loving friend. I've never complained and have always been there for you. I've continually been optimistic and still am. All I need is for you to communicate to me what is happening inside your beautiful self. Write or call me as soon as possible!

Your truest friend,
Matthew Ian

***

*"MOYERS: Do you ever have this sense when you are following your bliss, as I have at moments, of being helped by hidden hands?"*

*"CAMPBELL: All the time. It is miraculous. I even have a superstition that has grown on me as a result of invisible hands coming all the time—namely that if you do follow your bliss you put yourself on a kind of track that has been there all the while, waiting for you, and the life you ought to be living is the one you are living. When you can see that, you begin to meet people who are in the field of your bliss, and they open the doors to you. I say, follow your bliss and don't be afraid, and doors will open where you didn't know they were going to be."©*

## Friday, February 2, 2018

Dear Diary,

Yesterday morning after I finished student teaching the final chapter of *The Great Gatsby* at PDHS, I found myself traversing the staff parking lot once more. Talk about nostalgia! A month earlier, I began my tenure in Kyle Saad's English classes. Every day when departing the school I can't help but notice the gold Toyota parked in the same spot near the performing arts building that has my dad's name—JIM—in the license plate.

As I approached the vehicle, a six of clubs card appeared on the ground out of nowhere. I gasped, as I rarely find cards, though I'm always looking.

When I saw it there, I knew instantly what it meant: *Don't quit.* According to Robert Lee Camp in his book, *Destiny Cards*: *"When the six of clubs appears, you may have just discovered a special purpose to your life; one that is very meaningful and fulfilling. It is the card of responsibility to the written word as well as discovering one's personal or professional destiny."* © Then I realized that this same card is lying directly in front of the gold Toyota whose license plate reads "JIM."

But it gets even better. Last night, I had my first dream about Pops since his not surprising but unexpected death three days before Christmas. Now mind you, my last words to the old man were: "I've got to go. Call me tomorrow."

Standing in the doorway of his room at the old folks home, Pops smiled strangely, reached his left hand up to wave goodbye, appeared on the verge of saying something but never quite could. This poignant image, an exquisite metaphor, will forever be burned into my brain and memory.

In the dream, the phone next to my bed rang, startling me awake. Dazed and confused, I rolled over to my left side and picked up a beige rotary phone that looked just like the one we had in Cabazon when I was a kid.

"Hello."

And it's *him*—JIM—on the other end. Although it's staticky I heard him say… "Destiny, did you get the card I sent you?"

Bolting upright in my bed and wide awake now (in the dream), I clasped the receiver with both hands. "Yeah, I got it. I got it! Where are you, Pops?" He seemed reluctant to tell me so I leaned in a little more. "Where *arrre* you?" But he just sort of hemmed and hawed. Then the static suddenly increased and the line went dead.

I awoke with a shiver this strange Friday morning.

And as I brewed the day's first pot of medium roast in my eerily quiet, curiously bright kitchen thinking deeply about my vivid dream, the end of Fitzgerald's 1925 classic, released a month after my father's birth, was delivered suddenly from the womb of my purposeless splendor—

*As I sat there, brooding on the old unknown world, I thought of Gatsby's wonder when he first picked out the green light at the end of Daisy's dock. He had come a long way to this blue lawn and his dream must have seemed so close that he could hardly fail to grasp it. He did not know that it was already behind him, somewhere back in that vast obscurity beyond the city, where the dark fields of the republic rolled on under the night.*

*Gatsby believed in the green light, the orgastic future that year by year recedes before us. It eluded us then, but that's no matter—tomorrow we will run faster, stretch out our arms farther...And one fine morning—*

*So we beat on, boats against the current, borne back ceaselessly into the past.* ©

Or, should I say, rockets against the stars?

\*\*\*

## Saturday, November 12, 1994

My Dearest Destiny,

I've been real depressed the last week or so. Why am I so depressed? Because everything's dull without you! Nothing seems alive. Everything's dead and decaying. I feel like I'm walking around with nowhere to go. I fucking miss you, Destiny Jones. When we talk on the phone it all goes away but as soon as we hang up, the pain of this separation comes rushing back. We're 2,500 miles apart, madly in love, and all we can do is find an hour or two for one another a few times a week. It's hell.

Before, we were with together every day, ten to twelve hours a day, sometimes twenty-four hours a day when we got to sleep together. Before, we could make love whenever we wanted and now all we can do is use our hands and think of the other. Masturbation makes it worse. Every time I masturbate, it just makes me want you more. I realized the other night that masturbation sucks because after I come, you're not there in the flesh to hold, caress, kiss, and fall asleep with. It's like we're in a holding pattern anxiously awaiting the time when we're back in each other's arms. I crave you so badly. I want to sip cappuccinos with you everywhere and make love under the stars.

The phone just rang. It was Jamie. Every time the phone rings, I hope it's you. Every time I come home, I look for a flashing red light on the answering machine in hopes that you've left me a message of love. I love you so goddamn much. I think of you and my head spins with euphoria. I think of you and am sickened by the agony of your absence. I think of you and my cock gets rock hard like it is right now. I think of you and see a beautiful, charming, intelligent, special woman that I want to spend the rest of my life with and marry and have children with.

Yes, the rest of our lives is a long time, but the thought of being 50 years old with you is the greatest thing I can imagine. Nothing in my life would mean anything if I couldn't share it with you. I look at you and see myself. I see who I want to be. Look at our love for one another and our incredible compatibility. Why couldn't we die holding hands? I'm sure Dan and cousin Diana felt the same way. The rest of our lives does seem long but shit, that's because we're in our early 20s. We know nothing of age and time, but I'll say one thing: time don't mean shit because when I'm with you, there is no time.

Destiny, I do want to marry you. Let's just figure out what the fuck we're going to do and get some balance in our lives first. I want us to start our lives together so that we can bring some stability and yes, happiness to all the chaos that seems to follow us. The thought of living with you and sharing a bed, and a home, and a life, and my big dick with you every goddamn day is the greatest feeling ever!

That's what it is—a feeling I get all over my body. It's not a thought, it's a full-body feeling. When I'm with you everything seems right. That's how it was last October, and that's how it'll always be. You're it, Destiny. You are it! When I say that I love you, I hope you know it's true. Vanquish any doubt now! Let me love you, Destiny Jones, and see how the world will change.

It's 3:00 p.m. It took an hour to write this letter. I love writing letters because it's like I'm talking to you. Well, not exactly but a good substitute. I've got to go. I have to do some reading and I'm going to see your Pops in an hour or so. I'll talk to you in three hours. I can't wait. I love you, sweetie. Hang in there.

Your bestest friend,
Matthew Ian

P.S. Don't beat yourself up for coming home early. Who cares if you didn't finish the whole semester? I certainly don't. I can't wait to see you in just one week! When are we going to stay at the Sandman Inn? Are we going to Disneyland? Write me one last letter, beautiful.

****

# *The End.*

# *Epilogue*

Well, about six weeks ago, she heard the name Gatsby for the first time in years. It was when I asked you—do you remember? —if you knew Gatsby in West Egg. After you had gone home she came into my room and woke me up and said "What Gatsby?" and when I described him—I was half asleep—she said in the strangest voice that it must be the man she used to know. It wasn't until then that I connected this Gatsby with the officer in her white car.

When Jordan Baker had finished telling all this we had left the Plaza for half an hour and were driving in a Victoria through Central Park. The sun had gone down behind the tall apartments of the movie stars in the West Fifties and the clear voices of little girls, already gathered like crickets on the grass, rose through the hot twilight:

*I'm the Sheik of Araby,*

*Your love belongs to me.*

*At night when you're asleep,*

*Into your tent I'll creep—*

"It was a strange coincidence," I said. "But it wasn't a coincidence at all." Why not?" "Gatsby bought the house so that Daisy would be just across the bay. "Then it had not been merely the stars to which he had aspired on that June night. He came alive to me, delivered suddenly from the womb of his purposeless splendor.

—© F. Scott Fitzgerald
*The Great Gatsby*

# *About the Author*

Erika Lee is an NYU acting school dropout and 2011 graduate of California State University, San Bernardino, where she earned her *Bachelor of Arts* in English Literature. This milestone coming nearly two decades after she skipped out of playwright David Mamet's *Practical Aesthetics Workshop* at the Atlantic Theater Company in New York City. In addition to writing *Sex & Coffee*, her debut novel, she is a creative writing teacher who loves hot yoga and lives in Joshua Tree with her daughters.

www.ingramcontent.com/pod-product-compliance
Lightning Source LLC
Chambersburg PA
CBHW070319120726
47909CB00008B/2513